9 95

I AM NOT THE OTHER HOUDINI

I AM NOT THE OTHER HOUDINI

MICHAEL CONNER

HARPER & ROW, PUBLISHERS

New York, Hagerstown, San Francisco, London

FIRST EDITION

Designed by C. Linda Dingler

Library of Congress Cataloging in Publication Data

Conner, Michael.
   I am not the other Houdini.
   I. Title.
PZ4.C7532Iaa   [PS3553.O5118]   813'.5'4   77–11794
ISBN 0–06–010842–8

78 79 80 81 82 10 9 8 7 6 5 4 3 2 1

For Linda:

2 good
2 be
$\dfrac{4}{26\frac{1}{2}}$ got . . .

1.

The lights of San Metro seemed to pop on suddenly as Bruce Nukhulls flew inland from them, toward the east. Nightfall came quickly here, he thought. And there was land—an entire continent, spread out beneath him in the darkness. He had to keep telling himself that there was no need to fear ocean storms: At home, in Washington, D.C., a short hop—less than one hundred fifty kilometers—put him over the cold, choppy Atlantic. Here he had flown nearly that distance northeast from his base at the Santa Cruz Preserve and to think that there was land beyond the mental boundaries of that radius offended his sensibilities somehow.

These people here in the Western Region saw the last of the day, held to the cool evening longer than anyone else on the continent. Surely that was one reason for the difference in temperament between both coasts of the Confederation, the predilection of the Westerners for the more accessible practices of Oriental philosophy. Wait. It will come. A damn annoyance to those accustomed to decision and immediate action. Nukhulls personally was of the opinion that the Confederation would be better off without the Western Region and their constant threats to leave what was left of the national fold. However, he had an assignment to carry out, and a theory of his to test. In that light, it made no difference to Nukhulls whether he traveled east or west. If only he could remember that he was over *land* . . .

He was grateful for the scattered lights which served as ground references: after all, he could be over Nevada right now, where direction could sometimes become meaningless until daybreak. Banking slightly, Nukhulls eased back on his stick a little. His controls were sluggish in the January air, however—he felt the change of speed in the pit of his stomach. Ten minutes east from Alcatraz beacon was enough, he judged. Holding his wrist up in the cockpit light, Nukhulls switched his wrist Finder to continuous reading. Its tinny warble informed him that the man in whom a tiny transmitter had been implanted five years ago was within a kilometer's spherical radius.

"Good shot, my boy," Nukhulls whispered, sucking cool air in between his teeth. This had to be it. After six weeks of tracking down false leads, reading false signals, grabbing the shoulders of the wrong people, he was now actually close to his old partner. Nukhulls let his hopper hang still in the darkness, smiled to himself, then switched on his spotlight. He thought about how easy it was to make plans as opposed to executing them. Which, he wondered, was the more rigorous test of the imagination? He looked at the few house lights directly below. This area had once been a residential suburb of San Francisco and Old Oakland, before the earthquake of the 1990s, before the Chinese tactical attack of 2023 and the systematic destruction of that ancient nation by the forces of the now defunct United States. Twenty-five years of war, which ruined a very well set up national system, a war that resulted indirectly at least in the forced depopulation of some of the largest cities in North America. What was left was a weak confederation of energy-poor regional enclaves gathered beneath the molting wings of the aging hawk, President Lenore Houseman.

Only the West, it seemed, had escaped, persisting on a combination of agriculture and technological industry, fed by an ingenious network of cottage craftsmen and all sorts of power generated by anything but petroleum. Underneath him, Nukhulls knew, lived salvagers, truck farmers, and more-scientific types who grew semiconducting crystals in garage vats. His Finder beeped again, more loudly, indicating yet another type who thrived in the underside of the regional economy:

Psychokinetic operatives.

Nukhulls twisted back on his stick and let the hopper settle down slowly. In the spotlight, it looked like trees had overgrown whole neighborhoods. Swinging about fifty meters to the north, he found a break in the center of a paved cul-de-sac. There were no house lights in the general vicinity, for which he was glad. The people here were reputedly ill-disposed toward strangers, an attitude which had served well when San Metro had closed its borders and the periphery was crowded with clamoring stragglers who had survived depopulation in other, less fortunate urban centers. Naturally, he had come prepared to counter any such territorial outbursts. There was his hand crystal, always handy for quick inside work, and, if necessary, all his hopper power could be directed to a short-term antipersonnel field strong enough to stun all but the most determined attackers. But Nukhulls did not intend to use these weapons. He wanted to get in, find his man, and get out, smoothly and without a sound. Plans and execution again. Cursing his own nervousness, he set his machine down and cut systems, finally presetting his controls for a fast takeoff. Then he got out a small plastic snap case and a flashlight from behind his seat. One deep breath; then he popped the hopper bubble and stepped outside.

Ah, the night breeze, which sorts and selects those branches it shakes . . .

There were six other houses on the court; Nukhulls illumined each one briefly. Five of them looked as if they had not seen use for fifty years, and in a country prone to minor quakes, subject to pounding winter rains, and baked mercilessly in summer, disintegration came much sooner than that.

3

Porch awnings had collapsed across doorways; window glass was long gone. A child's tricycle lay crumbling and twisted on the broken driveway just to his left. A tree stump bore the marks of an unsuccessful ax attack. Huge thistles, some new, some of the color of mud, predominated.

But the house at the end of the court appeared to have benefited from some regimen of repair. Where glass was missing, patches of cardboard and plywood had been nailed in place. A path had been beaten through the weeds to the front door. The Finder reading confirmed the visual impression. Ryan Arcad was somewhere inside that house. Holding his arms close to his body, Nukhulls started for it.

Something warm and heavy bumped against his ankle, startling him so much that he flung his crystal away. "Damn!" he said, breathing softly, shining his light down on a large orange cat, which glared at him and did not move. Conceding the feline's position momentarily, Nukhulls swept back the weeds on both sides in an attempt to locate his weapon, but the search was futile. It would be hard to find a man in those weeds. He gave up, pushed the cat aside almost politely, and continued on his way. The fact that he was without his favorite weapon disturbed him a little. There was, after all, no telling what Arcad's frame of mind might be. But Nukhulls still had his dead-man—a homing laser, which had been surgically implanted below his left pectoral muscle. It was a weapon designed specifically for use against psychokinetic opponents, and in theory it was a great idea. Should he be subject to any kind of compulsive energy, the weapon would be triggered by the relaxation of his sphincter muscles. In practice, however, it had not worked too well. Several neat holes in Nukhulls' bathroom wall attested to that fact. Nevertheless, he activated it now, hoping that it would not be tested tonight.

He pushed open the front door of the house. The air was stale, not with dust but with the smell of dirty clothing, grease, and onions. The Finder display on his wrist indicated that Arcad was within ten linear meters. Nukhulls played his beam around the room. There was a stone fireplace clogged with the ashes of recent fires. The floor was partly covered with a ragged carpet; in other places, tiles had been stripped away from the slab floor. A few books, some open and lying face down among shards of linoleum, served as coasters for tilted, empty bottles. An ax, scattered kitchen matches, some rumpled clothing, more bottles—there were too many bottles, lined up against the wall, on the mantel, some smashed among the fireplace ashes—told the rest of the tale. Arcad had been drinking again. He was still trying to forget what he was.

There was a hallway to the right, which led past a bathroom and on to a couple of bedrooms. Now he felt a tingling at the base of his skull, something he had not experienced for five years—since the last time he had seen Ryan Arcad. In all the time Nukhulls had known the man—and their association went back almost twenty years—Nukhulls had never been able to tell whether the sensation was a purely subjective reaction to his presence or a result of some kind of mental static involuntarily projected by Arcad's brain. Whatever it was, Nukhulls could never quite quell the feelings this loss of self-control produced. It was, quite simply, fear. It was not an emotion Nukhulls preferred; he hoped that the technicians had not set the trigger too finely on the reinstalled dead-man.

The first bedroom was piled with cords of wood neatly cut and split. Nukhulls opened the door to the second bedroom slowly, just as his flashlight beam caught part of a body prone upon a mattress on the floor. An open book shielded the man's face, as if the reader had passed out in mid-sentence. Nukhulls saw that the book was something by Ouspensky. This had to be Arcad! Now he considered: The plans were set, and all he needed was this unconscious man. Still, it was hard to ignore the feelings of pity which competed with his sense of duty and with his own very personal needs. Arcad made a good agent and was a very special person, but he was desperately reluctant. The whole of his adult life had been devoted to the negation of the very powers which made him so different from

5

everyone else. It seemed that here, in this corpse of a suburb, Arcad had achieved some kind of peace, however alcoholic it was. For an instant, Nukhulls could almost believe that nothing was worth disturbing this man.

Yet, his own plans remained.

He shined the light down on Arcad, mumbling what passed for an apology. Gently he nudged the book from Arcad's face and was startled at how the man had aged. He was thirty-seven but looked over fifty. As Arcad stirred under the light, Nukhulls wondered if he'd be able to drag him all the way back to the hopper. That wasn't decent, and in any case there was always the chance that the psychokinetic would wake suddenly and make things difficult in the close confines of the two-man hopper. Therefore, he took the plastic case from his belt, got out the hypo and a vial of parogen, a strong stimulant which, in Arcad's case, had the curious effect of subduing some of the man's more formidable brain centers.

"It's not yours to kill," he said, jabbing the needle home.

Arcad stirred again, moaned, and lifted his head. Nukhulls shined the flashlight onto his own face. Arcad winced, shaking his head as if his eyes refused to focus properly.

"Who—" he started before the pain took him. "Ohh . . ."

"Can you see my face, Arcad? It's me, Bruce Nukhulls."

He shook like a drowning man suddenly; Nukhulls chose to pin his shoulders until the thrashing subsided.

"Simmer down, simmer down, you'll be all right in a minute." The tingling in his own head diminished, an indication that the parogen was going to work. "There you go, that's right, take it easy." He retrieved the flashlight with one hand while brushing Arcad's damp hair back from his forehead with the other. "No one's going to mess with you, okay?"

"Let go." When Nukhulls backed off, Arcad rubbed his face furiously with the heels of both hands. "Oh my god, I don't believe this."

"Believe it and say hello."

Arcad stared. His eyes were the color of adobe bricks, and

Nukhulls had always had trouble facing them. Not that he was afraid of recrimination, nor was he inclined toward guilt. It was just that there was something so lost about them, so lacking focus and definition that old bearings could become scattered very quickly. Finally, though, Arcad extended his hand. Nukhulls helped him to his feet.

"That's more like it! How've you been, partner?"

"Drunk 'til just now." Searching through a pile of debris by the foot of the bed, Arcad extracted a cigarette and lighted it. He shook his head through the smoke. "Sorry, I just don't comprehend the situation at the moment."

"Drinking," Nukhulls said, nudging an empty bottle with his toe.

"There's not much else to do out here."

Nukhulls allowed himself anger now. "Don't hand me that!"

"If I'd known I was in for an interrogation this evening, I'd have prepared some suitably witty repartee. At the moment, though, my head's splitting, so if you'd just go away—"

"Still kidding yourself. Suffering nobly amid the empties. By the way, who does your shopping for you?"

Arcad seemed embarrassed momentarily.

"Your power's a lot easier to use when it's to your advantage, isn't it? Shit, I remember how it was when you left: 'I'm going to kill myself,' that's what you said, didn't you? And I didn't try to stop you. Want to know why?"

"Not particularly." He blew a couple of ragged smoke rings toward Nukhulls.

"I didn't stop you because I knew it was smoke." With a sweep of his hand he destroyed what Arcad had made. "Like this. We've all got a drive toward survival. Yours is particularly strong. Even though you pretend to reject your own nature, you still recognize it for the precious commodity it is. Otherwise, why not do the job yourself? You've, shall we say, restructured other minds. Why not alter your own, make yourself normal."

Arcad grimaced wryly, finishing the last of his cigarette

before responding: "You've come all this way to analyze me."

"No. I came because I need your help."

"Forget it. Get somebody else."

"If there were anyone else, I'd have got him."

"I still have your promise. You said never again after the last time."

"Oh, shit!" Nukhulls slammed the flashlight angrily onto the top of a bedside table. "You still won't admit those two snakes needed killing! They were going to assassinate two hundred and fifty congressmen—"

"That's not the point! You put me in the position where I'd have to kill them or be killed myself. Nobody tried those men! Nobody gave me the right to decide that—"

"They were going to detonate an explosive in the chambers of Congress. Two against two-fifty—it's simple arithmetic, for chrissakes!"

"And what's the equation this time?" Arcad shouted.

"None, dammit!" Nukhulls struggled to calm himself. "Just listen for a minute. This isn't anything big. I just want you to find out something, that's all. It's there and back. I need your finesse, Arcad. Nothing more should be required."

"Suppose I believe you. Suppose I help you? Do we go back to the old game? I mean, how long do you expect me to keep running?"

Until the battery in your Finder transmitter runs down, Nukhulls thought, dampening his smile. "We'll leave it open," he said. "You like to work, I know it and you know it, and maybe you'll want to stay on. Maybe you'll want to resume what passes for your retirement. You're a delicate instrument, Arcad; I'll leave it up to you."

Saying nothing, Arcad stared out the window until finally Nukhulls sighed disgustedly.

"There's something else in the world besides your almighty conscience, you know. Think about me. We were friends, remember? I've trusted you with my life, and you've done the same. So you moved out without a word—do you have any idea what I felt like?"

"Like you had to work a lot harder."

"Yeah, laugh about it. The fact was and still is that I care about you—you, Ryan Arcad—and I'll be damned if I'll let you rot away in the weeds when there's things that need doing!"

Arcad turned with affected dignity, holding himself up like a washed-out savage. "Look. Maybe I'm sorry about the way I ended things. I realize that you've always given me a funny kind of respect, like you didn't quite understand but were willing to go along with me, and I've always appreciated it. But the fact remains that we are through. I'm retired. As far as the Confederal government is concerned, I never existed anyway, so let's keep it that way. You're welcome to stay as long as you like." He bent down to scratch the orange cat, which had joined the two men, giving Nukhulls plenty of room. "I've got my cat to keep me company. This is George. You tell him there's nothing I can do."

"I'm giving you a chance right now to reconsider."

"There's nothing more to talk about."

Nukhulls was very close to feeling sick. He hadn't wanted things to go this way, and now, with Arcad backed into a corner, there was only one thing left to do.

"Ryan, I can't leave here without you. I've only done this once before, when I had to drag you out of the Capitol—"

For the first time, Arcad's eyes opened completely.

"I'm sorry," Nukhulls mumbled. "This is for Mother." He said the word slowly, with the pitch rising at the final syllable. Arcad gasped, stiffened, then lurched over, knocking the flashlight from Nukhulls' hand as he fell. He lay paralyzed, completely in the grip of involuntary catatonia produced by the maternal noun. Nukhulls felt strange, ashamed in spite of all the justification he had laboriously worked out for himself over the years. There were pangs of conscience mixed with the thrill of control, a feeling of power bordering on the sexual.

This must be how Arcad felt when he used his mind to change things! Isolated experiences like these made it harder for Nukhulls to understand how Arcad could ever refuse to exercise such control. It made him respect Arcad's courage and feel contempt for his caution.

For a man of Nukhulls' direct nature, this collision of attitude was too disconcerting. He shook his head, collected the hypo kit, and clipped the flashlight to his belt. The job of dragging Arcad outside was something else again: the man was fifteen centimeters taller than Nukhulls and a good twenty-three kilograms heavier. And he was unable to cooperate. Nevertheless, Nukhulls managed somehow to get him back through the weed path, lean him up against the hopper, and rock him over the side like a heavy wooden beam. Nukhulls felt George bump his ankle again; the cat looked up at him and meowed inquisitively.

"He'll be okay. Go on, I'll bet there's plenty of mice around."

George refused to move. Nukhulls was about to kick him away when, on impulse, he bent over and gathered up the surprisingly heavy animal. George went into the back of the hopper along with Arcad.

There was the stirring of bare branches overhead. Nukhulls caught the contempt frozen in Arcad's eyes and felt weak. Ignoring it as best he could, he sealed the bubble, setting a course for the Confederal Compound at Santa Cruz.

Then he closed his eyes and wearily sat back as the hopper suddenly lifted away.

2.

The Confederal Compound was ostensibly a radar base built upon the site of an old Nike missile battery located deep in the Santa Cruz Mountains. Presently it served as an indication of Confederal influence in the Western Region, and as such it wasn't much of a garrison. However, it served Nukhulls' present needs quite nicely: it was remote, fairly well equipped, and, on the surface, completely free of western interference. The bored garrison commander had been more than happy to accommodate an agent of the Department of Defense, and Nukhulls had been able to convert an empty dispensary to a congenial holding cell where Arcad could cool off and think the situation out properly.

Early the next day, the security guard nodded curtly to Nukhulls as he went in to check on his charge. Inside, all blinds had been drawn, and in the scant light Arcad could be seen stretched out on top of his blankets on the bed. He would not have looked out of place on a bier, thought Nukhulls, even though the catatonic grip had been released over five hours before, and the camp physician had assured Nukhulls that his man's physical condition was good enough—considering all the factors.

It was time to try again. Nukhulls reached for the blinds

closest to Arcad's bed, pulling them open sharply. Arcad blinked his eyes.

"Morning, Dracula," Nukhulls said, chuckling.

Arcad glared at him.

"Come on, it's a new day. Give me a break."

Arcad sighed finally, sitting up. "Where are we?"

"Deep in the wilds of Santa Cruz, such as they are. In the dispensary of the Confederal Compound."

"Well, we gotta go back. My cat—"

"Is sleeping peacefully between your feet at the moment."

"I'll be damned." Arcad stroked George's silky fur with the back of his hand; Nukhulls felt just a little smug.

"Now, you have to admit, a man who loves animals isn't all bad, eh?"

"You have me there, Nukhulls." Smiling, Arcad stood up and went over to the basin to splash water on his face.

"How about some breakfast?"

"After that double whammy you served up last night, I don't think so. Besides the fact that I don't eat in the morning, generally."

Nukhulls watched him scrub his teeth with the fleshy part of his index finger. "Well then, what say we let George finish his nap while we take a little walk?"

Arcad eyed him suspiciously. "What for?"

"You said you'd give me a chance—"

"You said it. I couldn't talk until a few minutes ago."

"Tell you what. You listen to what I have to say—all of it—and then if you don't like it, you're free to go."

"It's nice to know you haven't changed much." He wiped his face with a white towel.

"Why, thank you. Your clothes are on the nighttable."

Arcad looked at the new denims. "Those aren't mine."

"Yours were a little—"

"Neglected. All right. Turn your back."

Folding his arms, Nukhulls did as he was told. He would have to try not to get ahead of himself now. Hopefully, the soldier would be waiting on the northern perimeter with the little surprise Nukhulls had prepared. . . .

"Okay," Arcad called, "I'm decent. Let's go." Nukhulls followed him out, noting that the psychokinetic was still stiff from the seizure the Mother key had produced the evening before. The effect was comparable to a gigantic muscle cramp that was not, however, limited to any one set of muscles. Arcad was evidently in some pain, but he said nothing; Nukhulls decided it was best for Arcad to walk it off himself. Any verbal encouragement might lead to an argument.

Anyway, the day was gorgeous. The trailing end of a midwinter storm had left the sky a deep blue with a few puffed clouds clinging to the tops of the surrounding mountains. Out to sea—which was visible through a gap to the southwest— everything was clear. They walked silently northward, along a gradual rise that led past barracks and a motor-pool garage until at last they reached a knoll overlooking the entire base. Arcad was puffing a little, but the man wasn't the physical wreck Nukhulls had first feared he would be.

"This is a nice spot," Arcad commented, crouching on his heels. "Too bad the government's here."

"They might not be here too long."

"What are you talking about?"

"You don't make a habit of reading the papers, do you?"

"Papers are good for lighting fires."

"You should make more of an effort to keep up. This region's been getting the jumps as of late. They've been threatening to secede from the Confederation entirely, and that, my friend, would make a Confederal outpost here rather unwelcome. Look at the logistics: It's a perfect staging point for attacks on San Metro. Then, to the east, those lovely, fertile agricultural valleys. To the west, control over shipping lanes. With the personnel Washington has here, we might make a fight of it, but we wouldn't last long."

"Not to be rude, but I don't really give a shit."

"Well then, what about civil war? This country's been

through too much these last forty years, and especially since the depopulation. Things are just getting going again, and now it looks like we're in for another slaughter of innocents, to put it dramatically. D.C. has retreated as far as she will go; Houseman is committed to maintaining the integrity of the Confederation. The idea is unity at all costs. Am I making myself clear?"

"I'm beginning to understand your interest." Arcad stuck a peg of crabgrass into the corner of his mouth. It was a gesture of skepticism Nukhulls ignored.

"You remember how they didn't quite know what to do with me in Washington? You know, if it isn't bombing, or catapulting reams of position papers, they get a little uncomfortable. But I'm beginning to bring certain people around. Propaganda's my line now, Arcad. It's very much easier to control events through people making what they think are their own decisions, and right now I'm being given a chance. Houseman knows there isn't any other way, short of war, and the East hasn't the will or resources to carry a fight across the continent, though they'll be damned if they won't try. The people in command out here know what's going on, and that makes them arrogant. Too arrogant, I'm afraid. They'll go through with what they think is right, civil war be damned."

"And I suppose you think I'm going to change all of this—"

Nukhulls laughed. "Whoa, slow down there, boy! I mentioned yesterday that your part in all this will be relatively minor. A little intelligence work is all I need from you. And this will be something you'll enjoy. Have you ever heard of Alphonse Sterling?"

Arcad's expression remained unchanged, which disappointed Nukhulls a little.

"Should I?"

"His stage name is Houdini."

"Oh, the magician. Yeah, I may have seen him on the screen a time or two. What about him?"

"He's just signed to do an illusion for the nationwide broadcast that's to take place on the Fourth of July. So far, he's kept everything under wraps—he won't even submit an expense budget—and the fear back East, and it's my own fear too, is that he's got something up his sleeve. Something that might interfere with what we want to do during that broadcast."

"So?"

"So, we have to be ready. I don't want some scam artist triggering the events we were just postulating. I want you to find out what he intends to do, and why. And that's it."

"You know I can't read minds," Arcad said, spitting out the well-chewed blade of grass. "How the hell—"

A battle scream from behind interrupted him, and Arcad whirled to face a Confederal soldier, who charged with bayonet unsheathed. The response was instantaneous: Nukhulls saw the flash of concentration on Arcad's face, and the soldier halting immediately thereafter as if spitted. Struggling and confused, he turned his face slowly to one side. Arcad knocked him over with a single backhand blow.

"All right, all right!" Nukhulls grabbed Arcad and pulled him back. "A little slower, but still magnificent! You okay, soldier?"

The private shook his head. His face was red where Arcad had struck him. "Yes . . . I'm all right. What happened . . . sir—"

"Never mind. Go see the OD. He's got a pass for you. Just keep your mouth shut, hear, or you'll be clearing poison oak off the county road for the next six months, got that?"

"Yessir!" Collecting his gear ruefully, the boy gave Arcad one sidelong glance before sprinting full stride down to the main part of the compound. Arcad stared after him.

"Oh, no, you can't read minds. But there are other ways, aren't there?"

Helplessly, Arcad dropped his hands. "Damn you," he whispered. "God damn you."

Nukhulls slapped him on the back. "Let's go to work!"

He ordered lunch for both of them in a conference room where a projector and a video playback unit had been set up. The grilled-cheese sandwiches were soggy, but neither that nor the fact that he had been outmaneuvered seemed to affect Arcad's appetite. In fact, he also ate the portion Nukhulls himself could not finish. Out of remorse, and against his better judgment, Nukhulls allowed Arcad a single can of beer, which he drained off in disconcerting fashion. When the psychokinetic finished, Nukhulls dimmed the lights.

"What're these? Shots of you flaying live trout on your last vacation?"

"Shut up and look."

Suddenly onscreen was a man of about forty, with short curly hair framing a large forehead and round eyes set slightly too far apart. A firm mouth and finely sculpted nose retrieved an over-all impression of handsomeness. Even so, it was the eyes which gave the whole its undeniable character.

"Cute," Arcad remarked dryly.

"You should look so cute. I don't know how familiar you are with this guy. His complete background is with the stuff in the folder, so I'll summarize. Back East he may be known as just a magician, or just an entertainer, but out here he's a pretty big man. His following is definitely bigger than his profession. An interesting history. Came out of Chicago during depopulation, somehow made his way out here when the Metro was locked up tight. That's when they had the charged barriers and the patrols looking to shoot to kill, along with the death penalty for anyone caught inside without a resident's ID, or for anyone aiding and abetting such, et cetera."

"Lovely people."

"It's the reason they are where they are today, let me tell you. Anyway, Sterling got in with the help of a girl named Kam Simpson—married her afterwards. They laid low for a couple of years, dodging Metro security, then all of a sudden he started doing his act out in public. They'd do four or five minutes of something in front of anyone who happened by. Security went crazy trying to catch him, and pretty soon he was some kind of hero. People helped him get away. Here, look at this."

Nukhulls started the video loop, which seemed to be about fifteen years old, judging from the clothing worn by the people caught onscreen. The camera was positioned at the end of a BART platform. A small man—Houdini, though it was impossible to see his face clearly—dressed in a silver coverall and slippers jumped onto the tracks, and, after a few grand sweeps of his arms, was bound hand and foot to the rails.

"Who's the blonde tying him up?"

"That's Kam. Watch."

People waiting for trains peered curiously as Sterling went to work. Arching his back, Houdini wrenched his shoulders from side to side, as if caught in the throes of a claustrophobic fit. After a few moments of this exertion he sat up, wrists freed, and began working on the ankle cords. Just then a train rounded the station approach. Seemingly frozen for too long, Houdini suddenly threw himself forward, stretching out just enough for the train wheels to cut his bonds. Briefly, he waved to the horrified spectators, but by the time the train had passed, with security men already up on the platform, both he and his wife were gone.

Arcad whistled. "Not bad."

"You can imagine what Metro government thought about all this. See, he was doing this stuff three and four times a day for almost a year. And this at a time when they were telling people that their survival depended on not letting a single refugee in. No relatives, no friends, not even former residents. A lot of those people who felt screwed by this policy latched on to Sterling's cause. For once, a governing body showed some sense: rather than blowing their whole policy by coming down hard on a local hero, they incorporated him. One day Kam and Sterling were caught downtown. Instead of being put away, though, they were given residency. The

17

aiding-and-abetting charges against the local girl were dropped. Sounds like a happy ending, right? Well, guess who the Metro chairman was who made that wise decision."

"Couldn't tell you."

"It was Peter Deliewe."

"You mean the guy who's regional governor now?"

"One and the same. The two of them have been very close ever since. You might understand this: it's always easier to work together, even if the goals are different."

"Your acumen remains unimpaired." Arcad was groping the empty plate atop the coffee table. "Is there any sandwich left?"

"Sorry. I can get you another—"

"Never mind. So, there's Sterling and Deliewe supposedly working together right now, planning something nasty for your broadcast. Once again—why me?"

Nukhulls placed a different loop in his machine. "Tell me what you think of this." Again the BART platform came on-screen, but this time the crowd was much larger and the steel awning was decorated with bunting.

"This was billed as an anniversary performance, last spring. You can see that Sterling looks a little heavier, but otherwise everything's pretty much the same. But watch."

Again the illusionist was tied down. This time, however, the train appeared before he had made a single move to free himself. Though there wasn't any sound, the open mouths indicated that more than a few people were screaming. Houdini remained oblivious to what was happening, until just as he was about to be run over. Then the front of the train was partially obscured by what seemed to be mist. The cars flashed by, and when they were gone—Sterling stood triumphantly alone on the tracks.

Nukhulls halted the tape and turned on the lights.

"Quite an improvement in technique, wouldn't you say?"

Arcad made no reply.

"Perhaps you can't verbalize it. Look. The first escape was all clear dexterity and timing. The man is an athlete. But the second . . . Tell me, how would a man like you explain it?"

"Maybe a dummy," Arcad said testily. "Or, you could have doctored the tape."

Nukhulls couldn't help laughing, but he did so gently, to avoid ruffling his partner's feelings any further. "Maybe someone did. I certainly did not. But let's say the tape is genuine. The way I see it, there're two possibilities. First is that he's on an incredible pitch, able to move faster than most of us can follow, given the distractions of the moving train, the people on the platform, even the lighting conditions. The second possibility—"

"No!"

"The second possibility is that somehow the man has power similar to yours. That he's a psychokinetic."

"That's not possible."

"Now don't start sulking—I'm offering speculation. And anyway, you're the last authority I'd accept on this particular question."

Arcad stood up angrily. "Still serving up the truth in bite-size chunks! I thought you said this was going to be a straight job. Finesse, you said—shit!"

"Ryan, it's precisely the reason I can use you, and only you. You're the only man I have who can protect himself against what Sterling may or may not be able to do. And it's still a simple thing. All you have to do is catch his eye, get his confidence. Find out if he really is like you. Get the specs on his illusion and how he intends to use it. Report back and I'll take the necessary countermeasures myself. That's not so tough. And admit it: Aren't you the least bit curious about Sterling? Wouldn't you like a challenge for once in your life!"

Arcad's exasperated expression betrayed the fact that he did, and he spoke a little more calmly. "All right, Nukhulls. And what if he does have what I have, and what if he's planning something bad—from your viewpoint?"

Nukhulls hesitated. The wrong word here could destroy the

spirit of cooperation he had so tenuously nurtured. There was still the Mother key, if things turned ugly, but that would make Arcad useless. There was only one mind capable of triggering the forces Nukhulls required: the conscious and cooperative mind of Ryan Arcad.

"What if," Nukhulls repeated.

"You expect me to wipe him out, don't you?"

"I ask only for information. Anything else is subject to your judgment in the field. As it always has been. I can't run everything myself. I certainly can't run you." Nukhulls waited, until he saw that Arcad was frowning petulantly. He was thinking of *details!*

"Jesus, this can't work! How the hell do you expect me to get close to Sterling? Materialize in the middle of his house?"

Nukhulls got out an old book bound in blue leather from a briefcase under the projector stand. "Something like that. Here, catch."

"What's this?"

"*The Autobiography of Robert-Houdin, Ambassador and Conjurer to the King of France.* I want you to look over the places I've marked."

"What for?"

Nukhulls walked away, pausing in the doorway. "Because therein, Ryan Arcad, lies the key to the heart of the Great Houdini." With that he turned and walked to his own room, whistling a nameless tune on the way.

For the next two days Nukhulls left Arcad completely alone. There was nothing to be gained from further prodding, and he wanted to give the psychokinetic time to absorb what would be his role in the situation, time for his imagination to work out a variety of scenarios. The result would be an Arcad completely assimilated, aware of ends, aware of means. Limits had to be established. For a man like Arcad, limits were essential: Great power maintained itself through knowledge of where and when it was going to be applied, and, more importantly, where it was not. Arcad had to get that clear if he was to be effective, and Nukhulls was more than happy to give him the chance to do it.

He saw him that first afternoon, walking head down along the perimeter, pacing the circumference which had been given him. What a strange man, strange even without the power which genes or chemistry had imposed. With his white hair, he looked like a stone ghost, and his face—who else had that twisting of features, betraying an inner struggle which didn't stop, never left him alone. Arcad was the essence of power in conflict with conscience: He understood that there was only one person to stop him, and that person was himself. Somehow he'd been able to find the character, the agility, and the unyielding tenacity to fend off all the lures, the inner games, the overt desire to let that power flow. Was he tired now? Would he ever give up? The consequences of such a surrender were something Nukhulls did not want to think about. There were too many bonds between the two men. God help the world. Yet Nukhulls did not let his concern for the global status quo interfere with his own aims. His needs were just as real as Arcad's—though admittedly less frightening. In the present instance, he did not view stopping Alphonse Sterling as any sort of holy quest; rather, he saw it almost as a businessman would see a competitor with a new and better product. The end became tripping Sterling up, and the means became *how* to pester, how to annoy, how to hinder. That *how*, of course, was Ryan Arcad—and the man had been correct: it was much easier to employ those special capabilities. But Nukhulls did not feel much guilt; certainly he didn't believe that this assignment in any way jeopardized Arcad's inner struggle. Indeed, it was their association that had built Arcad up, forced him to recognize what it was he fought, and gave him its measure and the wherewithal to hold on a little longer. Nukhulls could almost feel pride. He was protecting a reality, of sorts, and at the same time employing the energy thus thrown off as a useful by-product.

So, let the man get himself ready. Nukhulls had the time.

But not too much. The evening of the second day, Nukhulls went back to the dispensary. Under his arm he carried a green metal ammunition box. He rapped on the door and stepped in without waiting for a response. Arcad, in his shorts, was lying on the bed.

"I was wondering how long you'd let me rot."

"Not at all." He opened the box. "Care for a beer?"

"Sure." Arcad opened his and took a long pull—though not desperately this time.

"Feeling any better?"

"Yeah. I think I needed the fresh air."

"Good, good. Well, think you're ready to go?"

He shrugged. "Don't know."

As Nukhulls seated himself on a bedside chair, George jumped into his lap, settling quickly. Nukhulls flicked at his ears with a finger. "Okay," he said. "Let's start with the book. What did you think?"

"It was a little overblown, but entertaining. The man, if you can believe him, *was* pretty clever."

"Yup. You read about the handkerchief thing he performed for Louis Philippe of France?"

"The one where the scarves collected from the ladies in attendance were found in an old box beneath an orange tree? That was pretty good."

"And you understand the principle behind it?"

"I think so. A little sleight of hand with the scarves, then some applied psychology to get King Louis to name the location where Houdin's assistants had buried the box before the performance. Yeah, I liked the way he gave the king suggestions that either seemed too easy or were too far away to check quickly."

"Okay, you got the point. The one flaw in this effect is that the performer provides the list of places—which, if he isn't skillful, leaves the whole thing suspect. But, if the king had been allowed to rattle off some location off the top of his head, the trick could not have been successful, correct?"

"Naturally. But what's this got to do with the Western Region?"

Nukhulls grinned. "I'm getting to that. You are going to baffle Houdini with this trick. There's going to be a party at his mansion Friday night. I've wangled a couple of invitations, which wasn't easy, by the way. Usually there's a sort of amateur hour during these things, where his friends perform little tricks he's taught them. You're going to break in with this."

Arcad finished off his beer. "Yeah? And how am I going to do that?"

"In your own unique fashion, friend. We'll bring this box with us, work up the trick, and when Sterling names a location, you're going to put the damn thing wherever he says."

"Why use an ammunition box?"

"Two reasons. First, his house is at Devil's Slide, just south of Pacifica. It's an old shore battery that's been made habitable—cut right into the hillside, from what I understand. So, it's just possible that there are a few buried ammo boxes around—adds to the sense of wonder and mystery, get it?"

"Okay. What's the other reason?"

"We're adding a little coda to this trick. The object is to make him madder than hell—and to get you invited to stay on. How you're going to do that is up to you. But you'll manage, I'm sure." Nukhulls put down the box and took out the remains of the six-pack, pulling it away when Arcad reached for a second beer.

"Hey—"

"Just hold on a second. I want to see how you move this box."

"All right." Arcad made a grab for it.

"Not that way, for chrissakes! Do it with your mind."

"Is this really necessary?"

"It is if you don't want to look like a jackass Friday night."

Mumbling something, Arcad closed his eyes briefly. The box rose from the table.

"Where do you want it? I can put it someplace you won't like—"

"I want it under the bed, but not that way! It's wobbling like a blimp with morning sickness. Put it under the bed, zap, intact!"

"Man, I don't know if I can. . . ."

"Do it, god damn it!"

Arcad closed his eyes again, and this time the box disappeared. Nukhulls ejected George from his lap, stood up, and stooped to retrieve what had just been teleported. Never mind the tingling in his skull! Now both men were smiling. Nukhulls handed Arcad the rest of the beer.

"Kind of fun, ain't it? You know, Ryan, somehow I don't think that Alphonse Sterling will be ready for you!"

3.

"Just forget about the goddamned cat, will you. I've left orders, he'll be fed. I'll feed the damned thing myself, all right?"

"I was just worried about him, that's all." Arcad stretched out as much as he could in the small hopper. He yawned, and the glow from the green panel displays gave him an unsettling resemblance to an oversized gargoyle.

"Wants to bring his cat to a party . . ." Nukhulls swore an oath.

"You don't like flying at night, do you, Nukhulls?"

"Not when I've got you bitching about a cat and I can't get locked . . . wait a sec—" A tone sounded five times rapidly. "That's it. Five kilometers."

"You're positive it's the right one now?"

"You want to take us in?"

"No, no, you're doing fine. Just don't put us in the drink. I don't want to be found on the beach with a tuxedo on."

Nukhulls looked over at him, still amazed at the changes which had come over Arcad so quickly. He was perfectly shaved, and his silver hair had been cut in distinguished fashion, which, with the tuxedo, made him look like an oversized composer of the Schönberg school. He would cut a figure at this party, of that there was no doubt. Nukhulls, whose own vanity ran a little too deep, was disheartened by the contrast his own appearance made. His torso was too long and his legs were too short. Arcad had said that he looked like a bald ventriloquist's dummy, and he did almost feel like one. He would be part of the scenery tonight, with control in the hands of the man beside him, a man who had grown increasingly glib to the point of overconfidence.

Another high-pitched warble indicated that their ship was close enough for visual contact. Nukhulls eased back on the stick, straining for a view of the floodlit hopper pad just below. He floated down to a landing that wasn't all that easy—the pad was small, at the base of a steep outcropping of rock. Close on either side was a drop of three hundred feet to the Pacific Ocean. And it did not help that several idiots had left their machines parked on the landing grid.

Still, he managed. They taxied over rough ground to where most of the other hoppers were parked. Nukhulls cracked open the bubble.

"This doesn't look like much," Arcad said.

"Maybe not. But the top of the rock up there has the best look at the coast for fifty kilometers north or south. Which is why this used to be a shore battery during the Second World War. The blockhouse and gun turret are still in place—and see that steel tower? Original equipment."

Arcad got out of the hopper for a better look. Parts of the cantilevered frame that supported the observation platform were completely overgrown by wind-lashed cypresses. Their long, dark branches seemed to hold the whole thing up.

"It's the inside that matters anyway. Part of this rock was carved out for the original shore emplacement. Sterling completed the work. Come on now, we're late as it is."

"How do we go up?"

"This way. Watch your step."

An asphalt ramp, broken up by tenacious weeds, led to a concrete stairway that traversed the rock. The only handhold was a rusty steel cable strung through a series of skewed posts. At regular intervals the ocean boomed against the rocks straight down; and with the darkness and the phosphorescent foam, Nukhulls thought he could almost reach over and scoop up a glowing handful of water. Every forth or fifth wave sounded like an explosion.

"Jesus!" Nukhulls yelled. "Listen to that. I'd go nuts!"

"It's the eternal struggle, Nukhulls, water against stone."

"A waste, if you ask me."

"Come on, what've you got against sand?"

Without a reply, Nukhulls concentrated on reaching the top of the stairway. He was slightly more out of breath than he would have cared to admit. On the landing, a steel doorway protected what had been the entrance to the blockhouse. A small placard was bolted to the top of it:

YOU ARE NOT WELCOME HERE

Abandon All Entry
Those of You That Hope

(Invitations in Slot)

Nukhulls got both of theirs out, but Arcad stopped him from following the written instructions.

"Wait a minute. What about this stupid box?"

"Christ, almost forgot. Put it behind the shrub there."

"Okay." There was a rustle, and when Arcad stood straight again he was picking foxtails from the sleeves of his jacket.

"Think you'll be able to locate it when the time comes?"

"Absolutely."

"All right, then, let's go."

But again Arcad prevented him from depositing the invitations. Annoyed, Nukhulls turned toward him. Even in the wind, Arcad's hair, stuck fast with brilliantine, remained undisturbed. His stare was intense, almost threatening.

"I don't want anyone hurt. Do you understand me, Nukhulls?"

"That's up to you. Now, are we going in or not?"

Arcad released his arm; one by one, Nukhulls pressed the plastic slabs into the slot. Silently, the steel plate slid open to a bare concrete corridor. There was no sound except for the echo of the waves, and that was cut off as the door slid shut behind them. A hint of red light was just sufficient to guide them to the end of the corridor and a second, oaken door.

"Hell of a party, Bruce."

Nukhulls ignored him. "Through here, I guess. You going to be all right?"

"Right as rain in a drought."

"Remember what I've told you, then. Catch Sterling's attention. He's a proud man, so you might twist the knife a little. Just a little. You want to make him look foolish without it getting too serious, okay? Make the audience think maybe you're collaborating. That'll leave him an out, at least."

"With you all the way, coach." Without waiting for further advice, Arcad pushed the door open to the sounds of a large gathering. The noise diminished slightly when they entered. Immediately to the right of the door was a long bar; near that, a buffet table piled high with food. At the opposite end of the room was a small, circular stage. Soft regazz came from speakers on the walls. There were perhaps ninety guests, in various modes of dress, including, fortunately, formal wear. Nukhulls glanced at his partner: Arcad seemed to have shrunk slightly, as if the demands on his limited capacity for gregariousness were severely overtaxing.

"Pick up anything out there?"

"Not really. A lot of conflicting energy, like static on a radio, I guess. You know I can't read worth a damn."

"It's a shame you don't practice—"

A soft voice interrupted him: "Good evening, gentlemen." It belonged to a blond woman wearing a green dress. She smiled at them. Though she was not what could be called a truly stunning beauty, there was something about her—something in the way she carried herself, something in the color of her wide green eyes—which was disconcerting. And familiar . . .

"Hello," Arcad said shyly.

"My name's Kam. I don't believe I've ever had the pleasure," she said, eyeing Arcad a little more than cordially.

Lord, thought Nukhulls, so much for my advance intelligence.

"Pardon me. I'm Bruce Nukhulls. This is Ryan Arcad, my associate. We're friends of Senator Duenos."

"I see. Well, enjoy yourselves." She indicated the food and beverage service behind her. "Your pleasure, gentlemen; and have a good evening."

Arcad watched her move away. "Wow. So that's Mrs. Houdini."

"Meeting her, I'm not certain she'd appreciate the reference. But that's her all right."

"Hm. We didn't have a lot on her, did we?"

Nukhulls was now slightly embarrassed. "Not really, no."

"Well, perhaps she'll be of some use—in my getting an invitation to stay on."

"Forget what you're thinking. Stick to the plan. We'll both be better off." Turning to the bar, Nukhulls got a vodka gimlet for himself and a soft drink for Arcad, who sniffed it disdainfully.

"I'm on a short leash tonight."

"We're working. You should be half straight, anyway." Across the room, someone Nukhulls knew was making his way toward them. "All right, time to get lost."

"With me not knowing a soul!"

"I don't intend having our association burned on everyone's memory. I'll check with you after Sterling comes on."

"Sayonara."

"And watch the damned booze!"

Arcad winked, then drifted away, smiling and mumbling greetings with surprising expertise. When Arcad found a table for himself, Nukhulls felt free to look at some of the other guests. On the whole, there was a distinct air of western superiority, of the stamp which greatly irritated him. The feeling was not ideologically grounded; Nukhulls was simply averse to the kind of assertiveness that was in abundant evidence tonight. Over near the piano, for instance, a clique of artistic worthies held court. Behind the keyboard sat the oily and muscle-bound Kinchon, the transferist, who was one of the region's richest men. Behind him, rubbing his obscenely developed shoulders, was Jackson Rand, the elliptic novelist. Around them, flitting through the currents like social pilot fish, were three or four willowy young boys—or girls; it was difficult to tell for sure from this distance. But the entire tableau had obviously been set up for the benefit of the other guests.

It was difficult—impossible—not to be disgusted.

"Bruce Nukhulls!"

Nukhulls drank off the rest of the gimlet in order to mask his displeasure. The face he thought he'd recognized belonged, regrettably, to the man who had secured his invitations—The Honorable Jack Duenos, senior senator from the Western Region. He was a large, garrulous man and he smiled as he pumped Nukhulls' hand. What an arm he had! It had gotten him elected twice now.

"Hello, Senator."

"And you did make it after all! I was wondering if that stuffy little code book they give you back East would let you out to enjoy yourself."

Nukhulls forced a smile, while noticing the thin, goateed man standing behind Duenos. "Well, Jack, we don't fraternize with the natives generally."

"Still the same! Oh, excuse me, I'm such an oaf at these things. Bruce Nukhulls, this is Peter Deliewe."

"Ah, the regional governor." Nukhulls bowed curtly. "It's my pleasure, sir."

"Thank you." Deliewe's handshake was not enthusiastic, for he was obviously a man who took great pleasure in holding back. Probably he fancied himself deep and enigmatic. More than likely he was covering up a more mundane, but useful, political practicality.

"Bruce is with—what is it now, the Interior Department?"

"Defense. At the moment."

Deliewe raised his eyebrows. "Interesting. You're a long way from home, aren't you?"

By virtue of long practice, Nukhulls remained outwardly unaffected by the remark. Typical western gall, though! Did he intend to conduct a personal security check on a social occasion?

"I'm vacationing," he said calmly. "Taking advantage of your relatively pleasant winter weather."

"Oh. It's pretty miserable in the capital right now, isn't it?"

"I guess you could call a foot of snow one day and driving rain the next miserable."

Deliewe chuckled. "Personally, I prefer counting on rainy winters and nice clear summers. But, Jack, Mr. Nukhulls, please excuse me. There are a couple of young ladies who've extracted a promise of return from me. Perhaps we'll have an opportunity to talk later."

"Go, Peter, go. I'm sure you've got better things to do than chat with a couple of fat old men."

Nukhulls smiled after him. "Nosy sonofabitch," he growled, swirling the ice in his glass.

"Bruce—"

"Sorry. What's he doing here, anyway?"

"He never misses one of these things. You've got to understand, Bruce, we're a little more informal here. Peter can get more accomplished leaning against the bar, drink in hand, than in two weeks of scheduled conferences. You people can take a cue from him."

You people. Sometimes it was difficult to tell what set of political values Duenos held. No doubt it varied according to the situation.

"How about getting me another gimlet?"

"Certainly."

Nukhulls took advantage of the senator's absence to check on Arcad. He was still sitting alone at his table. From his expression it was impossible to tell if the psychokinetic was

31

amused, bored, or merely preparing himself. He had a drink, though, god damn him, and he'd better be able to handle himself—

Duenos returned, refill in hand. "There you go."

"Thanks. I suppose I ought to thank you for getting me in. This looks like a tough ticket."

"Tough for some. Who'd you bring?"

"Couldn't get anyone to come, believe it or not."

"Uh-huh." The senator had the knack of knowing when not to press. "So tell me, Bruce, how are things back in D.C.?"

"You don't bother going anymore, do you?"

Duenos laughed, deciding against taking offense. "Hey, I do all my voting by wire." He lowered his voice as he said, "Houseman wants me out here, you know that as well as I do."

"Uh-huh." Both men smiled.

"As a matter of fact, I just finished off an armed-services committee meeting before I got here. . . ." Nukhulls half-listened as Duenos rattled on about the situation in the Argentine. His attention was redirected to Arcad's table. Kam was now sitting with him, moving her hands in animated fashion as she spoke. Arcad could have been another piece of furniture. It was the hair, Nukhulls guessed, shining smoothly in the soft light, giving him a look of total disaffection, from her, from everything. At length, Arcad smiled puzzledly and shifted in his chair.

"You aim a little high, don't you?" Duenos said.

Nukhulls looked up. "Eh?"

"You're looking at the Man's wife! Now, I can probably fix something up for you tonight—but she's slightly out of our league, I'm afraid."

"Don't worry, just curious. She's really not what you'd expect."

"Listen, I wouldn't kick her out of bed for eating crackers."

"I don't mean that. It's—"

"If you really want, I can introduce you."

"We've already met."

"Really. Well, I think I know what you're talking about. She's regular. But she also sparkles. And let me tell you something: her husband is where he is today because of her. Smart as hell. She does all his illusions."

"Does?"

"You know, plots out the effects, gets the running time down, designs equipment. She's supposedly working on his big thing for July."

"Great." Nukhulls breathed audibly. He was glad that Arcad wasn't around to hear Duenos.

"What's that?"

"I said I think I'll get myself something to eat. Circulate a little. You must be keeping somebody waiting yourself."

"All right, Bruce, I won't tempt you to lie to me any longer than I have to." He turned, halted, then faced Nukhulls once more. "You know what you might do for me, though."

Nukhulls lifted his head.

"Find out what line your partner over there uses. He seems to have made quite a hit. *Salud.*"

Annoying though it was, Duenos' deductive skill wasn't really surprising. Even though the senator had achieved his position mostly though a relentless drive toward compromise, he was not completely without talent. And Arcad didn't exactly blend with the decor, either. He decided to advise him to stay away from Houdini's wife—when he got the chance.

That chance would not come for a while. Abruptly, the music stopped. As if fed by the music, the noise of conversation died down a few seconds later. The raised platform was suddenly spotlit, and a voice came from its darkened wings:

"Mineral water!"

A compact man, dressed casually in a sport shirt and dungarees, stepped onstage to hold a glass up to the light. "Free of infestation," he shouted before slugging it down. The savoring of the drink took a few private moments before he acknowledged his guests.

"Ah, good evening, everyone!"

Nukhulls saw that Kam had left Arcad and was working her way closer to her husband. Sterling frowned.

"What's the matter with you kulaks! Let's have an articulate response." He raised his arms. "Good evening, Houdini!"

Without thinking, Nukhulls, along with everyone else, repeated the greeting. There was something . . . not a definite tingle, as with Arcad, but *something*—a chill across the top of the room, perhaps.

"How are you, Houdini. Hope you are well, Houdini . . ."

Again Nukhulls found himself part of the chorus.

"May the gilded dust of a thousand cremated angels frost you, your possessions, and your heirs, Houdini!"

This attempt degenerated into laughter at Sterling's hurt expression. It was impossible to tell for certain if he had control over his audience. It could be power or it could be confidence. Whatever it was, Nukhulls was aware that this was a man who trusted his own instincts completely, a man who acted upon that trust without regard for "moral" considerations. How different from Arcad, in personality if not in essence.

Sterling shook his head. "No class, absolutely none at all. Leave enough wood lying around and all the termites come out. Well, enjoy yourselves anyway. I'll be available to each of you, personally, for counseling, and/or confession, if necessary, before the night is over. I may even tell a fortune or two. . . ." Twisting both hands, he fanned and flourished two decks of cards. He threw the right—and came up with a large silver fork; the left produced an even bigger spoon.

"Oh, yeah, I'm hungry all right, but this will never do." He swung both hands down, and when he brought them up the fork was bigger than the spoon.

"You can see what it's like around here." He crossed his arms behind his back, and when he brought them up he held two forks and a fanned deck in his right hand, two spoons and a deck in his left. There was something in his mouth, too. Sterling stuck his tongue out slowly, revealing a gold baby spoon. Then suddenly he put down the props and jumped down from the stage.

"Ah, just a moment," he said, evidently upset about something. Sterling found his wife near the buffet table, where he pointed with some agitation to a chafing dish full of rock salt. It wasn't part of the act. Nukhulls caught the words *supposed to be oysters* and saw Kam attempt to explain something to him. Her face was very red, and when she turned away, Sterling was pressed to control himself. He stared, pulled himself together, and finally remounted the stage. Nukhulls was relieved. With Sterling's reputedly hot temper, the illusionist might have left the party before Arcad had his chance.

But the Great Houdini was striving to continue. "Uh, sorry folks, a slight mix-up. Hey, I was going to show you something I've been practicing all week. Let's have those cards again. Really I only need a few, but they make you buy these things in sets."

His audience, still confused by the confrontation between husband and wife, laughed uncertainly as cards fell to the floor of the stage. Houdini took a pair of scissors from his pocket, then grasped a single card between the first two fingers of his right hand.

"I'm not sure how good I am at this. But here goes—" With a snap of the wrist, he sent the card spinning out of the spotlit area. It returned suddenly, but Houdini's lunge with the scissors was too late.

"No, really, this is called scaling a card. I throw it so it boomerangs back—hey, look, if I wanted to do it the easy way . . ." He picked up a card, cut it in half, and displayed the two pieces triumphantly. "Huh? Huh? Pretty good, no?"

"No!" someone yelled.

"All right, here, I know what my problem is. Bring up the house lights." Sterling squinted as they came on.

"And you thought you were at a party! Sorry, this will only take a minute, then you can have your precious darkness back.

35

Let me get another card here, that's right." He opened the scissors and held them that way.

"This doesn't really look professional, does it? Never mind, here goes. One, two, three!" He tossed the card again. It banked upward, and almost touched the ceiling over the bar before it returned. At the proper moment, Houdini snapped the scissors shut, cutting the card neatly in two.

"Thrilling? Am I right? Don't all clap at once. Who out there wants to learn how to do this? How about you, darling, you look like you're over eighteen. No? Maybe next year, then. Come on, who wants to make a total jackass out of himself so we can all have a good laugh!"

"I will!" came a voice from the darkness. Houdini frowned.

"Get a spot over there." The light encircled Arcad's table. He leaned back in his chair, a cigarette dangling from the corner of his mouth. Nukhulls thought he looked entirely too relaxed.

Drunk or not, Arcad had to be given his chance.

"Now who the hell are you?"

"Your apprentice—with your permission." As Arcad stood up, Sterling regarded him with something close to malicious glee. Here was an opportunity to alleviate the embarrassment produced by the argument with Kam.

"What do you people say?"

Arcad acknowledged the applause with a grave nod of his head.

"Very well, come up here. You're a striking man. Yes, that's right, step up. You're not the ambassador from the Detroit Pistons, are you?"

"No, Houdini, I'm a student of the art of conjuring."

"I see, Mr.—"

"Arcad."

"Mr. Arcad. And you want to learn how to scale cards?"

"Well, I would. But actually I have a trick I want to show you."

"You have a trick to show me! This works, doesn't it? I mean, it isn't 'find the ball under the cup'?"

"Oh, no." Arcad smiled stupidly in just the right way. "This is a good trick." Great, Nukhulls thought. Let Sterling get just overconfident enough to deserve what's going to happen to him. He was surprised that Sterling showed so little sense.

"A good trick. All right then, show us your good trick."

"Thank you." Arcad lit another cigarette. "Will the beautiful woman in the green dress—"

"Do you want me to sit down?"

"I thought you already were."

God damn him, he *was* drunk! But, with the crowd laughing, Sterling could hardly take offense. Arcad waited for the audience to settle down.

"No, stay where you are."

"Thank you. Proceed."

"Thank you. As I was saying, I'll need a scarf. The woman in the green dress—you're Mrs. Sterling, I believe—yours is lovely; may I use it?"

Kam stared, the tension hers to break. Half-smiling, she sauntered to the stage, slipped off the silk scarf, and handed it to him. Arcad held it for the audience to see.

"Now, Mr. Houdini—"

"It's Houdini. Plain Houdini," he said with a growl.

"Oh, sorry. Houdini. You're known to be an expert on knots; would you mind tying it in a distinctive way?"

"Okay." He hurriedly made four square knots, which made a tight ball out of the scarf. "How's this?"

"Fine. Young lady, will you examine this and try to remember the way it was knotted. Now, I'm going to cup my hands. Please stuff the scarf between my thumbs." Arcad held his arms out unsteadily as Kam followed his instructions.

"All right!" He shook his hands over his head, stopped—as if he'd forgotten some important step—then brought them down again, opening them slowly. The scarf was gone, replaced

37

by a small brass key. Houdini's smug grin disappeared; Kam looked relieved.

Arcad interrupted the uncertain applause: "Please, folks, I'm not finished yet. Oh, sorry, these lights are hot—will you excuse me?" Arcad took off his jacket, tossing it to the front of the stage. Nukhulls thought he recognized Duenos as one of the spectators there.

"Mr. Hidini. You are of course familiar with the grounds here."

"I don't drink coffee."

"Ha ha ha, that's good. But I'm referring to the area in and around your estate. Would you say you're familiar with it?"

"I know my way around."

"Okay, put your thinking cap on."

"It's at the cleaners."

"Then I suppose we'll have to do without it. I want you to imagine you had something valuable you wanted to hide in the vicinity, so you could get at it if you needed to. Where would that place be?"

Nukhulls could see that Sterling had recognized the trick, and his expression showed that he was of two minds: to end a charade that would waste a lot of time, or to go through with humiliating a stranger who had publicly insulted him. Ah, but the man *had* made the silk vanish. . . .

"That's very interesting Mr.—Arcane? Let me see. Oh, yes, behind the turret directly above us is an old cypress with exposed roots. I'd put it inside them."

"Very well." Arcad closed his eyes and tensed his body. Nothing happened, apparently, because he opened them with a look of surprise, then tried again. This time Nukhulls felt the tingling. He wondered if Sterling felt anything, because the illusionist was shifting a little onstage.

"Would you mind sending your heavyset employee—yes, the red-haired gentleman manning our buffet—to that spot with digging implements?"

Houdini was exasperated at last. "Now just a minute—"

Kam spoke up: "Go ahead, Rusty."

"Hey, we've got guests, and I don't want him wasting his time."

"Al," she said, and her voice was very smooth, "you said the man could do his trick. Let him finish."

"All right, all right, all right! Russ, get going." He smiled through his teeth at Arcad. "But don't take too long."

"You'll have to dig about a foot down," Arcad called after him. Always the showman, Houdini signaled for music and had the spots brought down. Let them fill their plates, get another drink. Don't have them standing around too long, thinking. There was uneasy laughter and animated conversation. Oblivious to all of it, Arcad stood with his eyes closed, swaying gently to the music. Nukhulls hoped he had enough left for the finish. . . .

After several minutes Rusty reappeared suddenly, holding the dirt-caked ammunition box away from his clean uniform. Houdini was incredulous.

"You actually *found* this up there?"

"Right underneath. A foot under, like the man said. It was weird, too. I dug around for a few seconds and couldn't find a thing. Then all of a sudden I hit this."

"No soft dirt? Signs of digging?"

Rusty rubbed his shoulder ruefully. "No way. That stuff was like cement."

"Okay. What we have here I guess is a military ammunition box, padlocked shut. We'll have to pry it open."

"Try this. A reanimated Arcad offered the brass key to Sterling, who reluctantly fitted it into the lock. It popped open. Arcad waved off the applause. Kam came up to open the box. Inside was her knotted scarf, and she beamed.

"Wait, there's more." She pulled out a small bundle wrapped in yellowed paper. Carefully, she undid the strings around it. Inside was a chrome .45 pistol. On the wrapper was a note, which she handed to her husband.

"Read this, dear," she said.

Projecting as much ennui as possible, Sterling said: "It's dated February 15, 1946."

"Go on, Al."

"Give me a chance!

" 'To Whoever Finds This:

" 'When I was a small child, my father took me to a performance of Mr. H. Houdini, who escaped from a packing case, a milk can, and a glass cabinet filled with water. He died three weeks after we saw him. Now I think of him constantly. . . .' "

Sterling broke off. He was angry, yes, but also affected somehow, as if grief, long masked, had been forced upon him again. Clearing his throat, he resumed:

" 'I know he wishes escape from death. He has asked that I place my service pistol, with two marked rounds in clip, along with this note, for a feat of magic which will somehow be performed here by or with a namesake. His message is love, and a promise of help. I was to inscribe each bullet with my initials, and I have done so.

"Signed 'Master Sergeant Alexander Mattley.' "

Sterling looked at the pistol. His voice was hoarse as he asked, "Anyone know how to work this thing?"

An elderly gentleman raised his hand.

"Here you go," said Sterling. "Take out the clip and give me the shells."

"Let me see. Yes, here's the release. This weapon's in fine shape!" He handed back gun, clip, and bullets. "You wouldn't want to sell it?"

"Get out of here! Well, there it is, folks. The initials A.M. on each one."

Very slowly Arcad raised his arms to beckon applause, which came. For Sterling it had to be a strange and unpleasant experience. To have to listen to cheers that weren't for him! Perhaps his lapse in judgment bothered him more. He had taken Arcad for a drunken fool. Nukhulls knew that Arcad had to keep Sterling from going over the edge now.

40

"Well done," Houdini said. "Now—"

"One moment more, sir. The note stated that a feat of magic was going to be performed. If the gentleman would be so kind as to reload this firearm for me . . . Thank you very much," he said, taking the loaded pistol from the gun expert and then handing it to Houdini.

"What's this?"

"I'd like you to back off a few paces and fire at me."

"Hold it! I don't know who the hell you are, but I do know damn well how many ways there are to gimmick something like this."

Arcad stifled a burp. His eyes were glassy. "Try it. There's two bullets."

"Okay, I will." He pointed the weapon at Arcad's feet and fired. People screamed, and Nukhulls himself was startled, even though he had shot such pistols before. Arcad stared dreamily down at the hole that had been blasted in the stage floor between his feet.

"You give a nice pedicure. Will you now aim a little higher?"

"By God, I ought to do it!"

"Please, I insist you do."

"Yeah, and who's going to lug out your corpse?"

"I *challenge* you."

Houdini turned bright red. He'd been challenged, but he didn't want to be responsible if anything went wrong. It was difficult for him to believe that anyone would dare put him in this position. It was almost a minute before he was calm enough to speak.

"Ladies and gentlemen, I have given this man a chance to withdraw. He insists, however, on challenging me to assist him in a very old and dangerous effect. Okay, the man has placed his life in my hands. Or in the hands of his own skill, I've no way of knowing. So, I will shoot at him. Afterwards . . ."

He stepped back dramatically, exaggerating his movements as if playing to a huge theater. His arm came steadily down,

41

then held to the horizontal, trembling slightly.

Kam moved between the two men. "That's enough, Al. Give me the gun."

Her husband looked around her. "Mr. Arcad?"

"Proceed."

"Al, you're angry!"

"Which makes no difference to either the gun or this man. Are you ready, Arcad?"

Arcad made no reply. His eyes were vacant, and his face was slack, displaying none of the concentration it would take to stop a bullet. Was he trying to commit suicide? On impulse, Nukhulls reached for the new crystal he'd been issued at Santa Cruz; the weapon felt strange in his hand, and he wondered whether he'd be able to wing Sterling with it if he had to.

But that would be the end of his plans. He let Houdini squeeze the trigger. The room seemed to explode. Arcad was blasted back and lay motionless at the edge of the stage. Sterling let the chrome pistol drop as Kam ran over to the fallen psychokinetic.

There wasn't any blood! With her help, Arcad was able to stand. He smiled weakly, revealing the bullet clamped between his teeth. When he spit it into his hand, Nukhulls saw that one of his front teeth had been chipped: Arcad had almost blown it.

"A.M.," said Kam, holding up the bullet.

Now everyone was cheering. Sterling, grasping his role in the situation, hugged Arcad while encouraging everyone else. Arcad had eclipsed the Great Houdini, and for now it was a fresh combination, a taste of the unexpected. Let everyone think they'd worked together—it would keep Sterling from being too angry and would allow Arcad a chance to get in closer. Now the two of them could deal as equals—if Arcad could manage to stay on.

But he was attending to that right now, onstage. He was very pale. Whispering suddenly to Kam, he ran away from the spotlights. Kam followed, but they didn't get too far. The sounds of his vomiting were plain enough to Nukhulls' ears.

Perhaps it was self-induced, or simply the result of too much alcohol—either way, the result was pleasing to Nukhulls. For the moment, it seemed that everything had fallen into place. He got ready to leave. Alone.

4.

Ryan Arcad was dreaming:

He sat alone in his room with nothing to do on a hot summer day. There was a pack of cards on his desk, which was against the wall opposite his bed. By looking into a mirror he could see the pack, and with his mind he began lifting the cards out of it one by one.

He got several cards in the air at once and had them dogfight around the chandelier. The queen of spades won, knocking all the others to the floor. From the fallen suits Arcad constructed a throne for the victorious queen, who looked awkward and less than regal in the mirror. But he set her down, smiling to himself at the way she tilted toward the knave of hearts, whom she obviously pined for. It was then that he noticed his mother in the doorway.

She'd seen it all. Just back from the sanitarium, supposedly cured of his "affliction," Arcad's behavior upset her greatly. She was a beautiful woman, with long silver hair and fine skin, but her emotions distorted her features. She screamed at her son, who looked up and saw not his mother but a snarling, metal-skinned beast. He reacted instinctively, squeezing with his power, concentrating so much that he was unable to comprehend her choked cries for mercy, for recognition, for *sense*.

The throne of cards collapsed. Arcad realized what he'd done and looked at her, intending to correct the damage. But his mother's head had become a nautilus shell, its end open toward him, her shrieking of his crime spiraling out and out to the world. Arcad tried losing himself in the darkness, but that did not bring back the sound of her either. So, he opened his eyes. Forced them open to morning.

Every muscle in his body ached. Arcad had these dreams whenever he drank; thus, he had developed a routine to release his night-wasted body. The knots loosened and he was able, finally, to relax. Not that he felt all that much better. He had done quite well last night, but the fit of vomiting had been a clumsy ploy. He put it to too much excitement and too much to drink, a combination which prevented him from thinking clearly. After all, there were other ways of securing an invitation—he hadn't had to make himself physically unable to leave!

In spite of his nausea, however, Arcad smiled to himself. He was slightly out of practice, but he was still a functioning professional. Abruptly, he got out of bed, walked over to the window, and drew back the curtains to a view of the cloud-covered, colorless Pacific. Directly below him was a huge outcropping of basalt, cracked and weathered, a center of activity for wheeling gulls and a few sea lions. The combination of motion and distance made Arcad dizzy, so he stepped away and contented himself with an examination of his more immediate surroundings.

There was a faint scent of honey in the air, which produced a strange galvanic sensation atop his stomach. It was a reminder that there had been more to last evening than just his illness. *She* had taken care of him, wiping his face with a warm washrag, rubbing his neck, saying things to him that he couldn't remember, though he wasn't sure that that mattered. He wondered how Kam Sterling had gotten him up here.

There was a wooden footlocker on the floor at the end of

the bed. On it were a couple of towels and his own tuxedo neatly folded on top of them. A note was pinned to his shirt:

A shower makes it all better.

K

It was a suggestion he took to heart immediately. The guest room had its own bath, through a doorway to the left of the bed. Arcad grabbed the towels and headed for it, pausing to look at the holo portrait of Houdini which hung above the light switch. The man's bearing—in the portrait at least—was impressive: eyes clear, skin ruddy and tight. An impression of mystery was produced by eyes which apparently did not focus on any one object. This Arcad recognized as posturing; but he wondered if he'd feel that way if things had gone differently at the party.

There was no need to be cocky. Not, at least, until he'd finished his job, because at the moment Arcad had no idea whether Sterling was capable of moving even a Ping-Pong ball with direct mental force. Arcad turned on the shower and stepped in, intent first on getting the brilliantine out of his hair. The sharp spray affected his aching arms wonderfully. He closed his eyes, letting his mouth fill with water. Gargling it, he shot it between his teeth in an arc, like a fish.

"Well, good morning!" came a voice over the sound of the water. Arcad nearly fell. Kam smiled at him over the top of the glass.

"Continue, please. Don't let me disturb you."

"Uh, thanks," Arcad mumbled. Her hair had been pulled into a tight bun, and she wore a peach-colored blouse unbuttoned at the top to reveal part of her freckled chest. As she did nothing but continue to smile at him, Arcad began furiously rubbing the bar of soap through his greasy hair.

"There's shampoo—"

"I'm fine, just finished." He would have preferred to stay under awhile longer, but he found it impossible to shower for a grinning audience. Carefully, he replaced the soap in its dish, wrung out the washcloth, and hung it across the shower head. Then he turned off the water and stood there, simply dripping.

"Haven't you forgotten something?"

"Not that I can think of." Where had all the bravado of the previous evening gone?

Kam held up the towels. "I think you might want to dry off."

"Oh yes. Yes, thanks." He took them and immediately wrapped one around his waist before stepping out. Raising her eyebrows, Kam turned her back to him.

"Go on, get dressed. I won't peek—again."

"Thanks." After drying his hair he began hastily pulling his clothes on.

"Care for some breakfast?"

"I don't think so. My stomach—"

She had seated herself on the edge of the bed. "That's right, you were pretty sick last night. Any idea what happened? You didn't have that much to drink."

"Not sure," he lied. "Nerves perhaps. Or maybe lead poisoning—I had that bullet in my mouth for almost a half hour."

"Mm-hm. That's just as well. Al wants to see you. First thing, he said. But then, he is a little rude at times."

Arcad allowed himself to feel some hope. Perhaps, if he was lucky, he'd be done this morning. He sat down beside her to put his shoes on, and as he lifted his leg his back touched her.

"I'm glad he wants to see me. That'll give me a chance to thank him for his hospitality."

"Oh, it's not him you'll have to thank for that. In fact, I doubt he'll let you thank him for anything. All set?"

"Yep." As he stood up and watched her walk to the door, he realized that it was difficult at this moment to concentrate on Mrs. Sterling's husband. In fact, Arcad's discipline was not developed sufficiently to eliminate her influence on him. Then too, there was something about her interest in him that wasn't quite right either. The attraction was there, certainly, but somehow it was ingeniously extended—emotions channeled toward useful results. Anyway, Arcad doubted very strongly that Mrs. Sterling was one to lavish her attention on strangers.

Nukhulls should have done his homework here, he realized.

"Right this way."

She led him down a wide, skylit corridor decorated with some large coffee plants and a few scheffleras. At the end of the hallway Kam stopped to press an elevator button.

"We're up in the living quarters right now," she explained. "Those doors lead to a couple of bedrooms and a small sitting room that's carved out of the old gun turrets. There's a picture window and a veranda that juts out over the rocks. Unfortunately, the weather here is seldom nice enough so we can use it.

"Downstairs is where we had the party. There's a kitchen, also a small gymnasium. Below that, which is where we're going, is the old powder magazine. Al's got a study there. And his collection, in what used to be our workshop." When the car stopped she opened the door for him.

"What's this about a collection?"

Kam looked at him coyly. "Oh, maybe he'll show you. You're pretty lucky as it is. Not many people get to the third level."

Damn, Arcad thought as he caught the scent of honey again, I wasn't sent here to deal with this woman!

They went through a door to a concrete hallway lit by two bare bulbs in the ceiling. It was very cool—though a ventilation system kept the air from being musty. On the right was another door of heavy steel, this one stenciled in faded yellow:

MAGAZINE

which Kam pushed open with a thrust of her hip. Inside were two other doors, one of which was secured by a formidable padlock.

"You know, Mr. Arcad, that was quite a show you put on last night."

"Thanks. I hope I didn't embarrass your husband."

"Embarrass him! Oh, my darling, he was mortified." The door boomed shut behind them.

"That wasn't my intent, I assure you."

"What was?"

"I guess I was a little drunk."

"And you brought your little box just in case!"

"Well, I am an amateur magician—"

She halted the explanation with a finger to his lips. "Save it. And don't let him jump on you right away—that's usually his way when he's been annoyed."

"Okay. Only . . ."

"Only what?"

"Why prepare me this way?"

"I don't like to see anyone bullied."

"And your husband is a bully?"

"He can be. But you'll do all right." She rapped at the door, calling: "He's here."

"Come in."

She opened the door for Arcad, indicating with a sweep of her fine hands that he should precede her. He was ready; he stepped inside. There Alphonse Sterling sat, behind a plain oak desk near the back wall of the room. Engrossed in some writing, he did not immediately look up.

Kam chuckled. "Here he is, Al. I saved him for you."

"Good." He still hadn't looked up. "Have you got anything to do?"

"I was thinking of getting a market order ready. Then again, I may take a ride."

Sterling stabbed out the remains of a thin cigar. "Don't ride off the cliff, okay?"

"Yes, sir. Have fun, you two." The door closed and they were alone. Sterling squinted at his guest.

"Arcad, is it?"

"That's right."

"Have a seat. I'll be with you in a minute."

So, he was supposed to squirm. Well, Arcad had patience enough to get over it, and he amused himself by looking at the plaques and memorabilia which made the room something more than a concrete hole. There were several prints of Houdini in various costumes. In one, the illusionist was shown standing next to a white lathe gazebo that was completely filled with Kam, who was wearing an outrageous organdy dress; Arcad thought that she might have been sitting on a swing. He opened his mind in an attempt to gain an impression that might be of some use, but he got nothing out of the ordinary. If anything, the man at the desk in front of him was slack, drained of the manic intensity he'd displayed at the party. His hooded eyes were gray and revealed nothing, which left Arcad slightly dismayed. At this moment, his field pay did not seem adequate.

Finally Sterling put aside his papers and reached for a frosted glass apothecary jar. He seemed lost for a moment, but then he laughed.

"I'm trying to figure out just what to *say* to you. I suppose we'll start with this." Opening the jar, he took out a little ivory spoon and with it shoveled a sticky brown mixture into the bowl of a briar pipe that he kept on a stand near his telephone. He tamped the load and offered it to Arcad.

"Kef from the North African Protectorate. Half Moroccan tops, half tobacco. This has to be hand cut daily, and it's good."

Arcad hesitantly clamped the stem between his teeth as Sterling struck an enormous wooden match against the side of the desk. He drew in as much smoke as he thought he could handle. It was too much, and he coughed painfully. Sterling, on the other hand, sat back and sucked slowly, closing his eyes as he blew smoke out his nose. The smell was sweet. Arcad took another, shorter pull before settling back himself. Sterling watched him until Arcad felt almost compelled to speak.

"I want to thank you for letting me stay."

"Couldn't track down your ride. I wasn't going to kick a sick man out in the middle of the night."

"Well, I appreciate it."

"Don't mention it," Sterling replied dryly.

The kef was strong, the stimulating effects of the tobacco boosting the reaction to the cannabis. Arcad damped the combination before it drugged him completely. All the same, the room seemed slightly cooler, as if the flow of convection had been reversed.

"Your . . . ah, wife . . . said you wanted to talk with me."

"She was right." Sterling leaned over the desk. "I'll come to the point. Who the hell are you?"

"My name's Ryan Arcad—"

"That I know. Maybe I should ask who the hell you think you are."

"I'm under arrest?"

Sterling seemed surprised. "No."

"Then your interrogatory tone is a little premature, I'd say."

"All right." Sterling got up and began pacing behind his desk. "Then maybe I should explain something to you. We don't know each other, do we?"

"No."

"I have these parties once a month, sometimes twice a month. I try to limit my guest list to friends, or at least to friends of friends. You understand why, don't you? I don't have time to waste with creeps. I don't like to be bored. I don't like to be embarrassed. I prefer being comfortable in my own house with a gathering of fellow spirits."

"That's understandable."

"Good. Now let me ask again. Who are you?"

"A friend of a friend." Arcad smiled.

"A friend of which friend?"

The psychokinetic picked up a little silver goose from the front of Sterling's desk. The intent was to stir the man up a little—but not too much.

"I think, Mr. Sterling, that in light of what happened, I'd rather not say. He didn't know what I had in mind."

Exasperated, Sterling tried another tack. "Okay, forget that. Why don't you tell me what it was you did have in mind."

"I wanted a chance to show you what I could do."

"You live around here?"

"Diablo. I've got a garden in the yard. I go after rabbits and squirrels in the daytime. At night I practice my stuff. You might say I'm an aspiring performer. My friend, who is a friend of your friend, thought I was pretty good."

"Well, he's wrong."

"I—"

"You're damn good."

At this point Arcad touched the tail of the little goose. Apparently it was a lighter, for a ruby-colored beam issued from its beak, blackening a spot the size of a dime on Sterling's desktop.

"Give me that! Put it to good use at least." The magician relit the pipe with it, but Arcad refused a third toke.

"All right, Arcad, I can see subtlety is wasted on you. You made me pretty angry. I've done some bad things when I've been angry."

"So what did I do wrong?"

"Wrong! Look, you don't go into somebody's house to make him look like an asshole. Especially, you don't go into my house to beat me at my own game. I wouldn't, if I were you."

"I think you might have—for the right reason."

"And what the hell was your reason?"

"Like I said. I wanted to show you what I could do."

"All right, all right! Jesus Christ, I can't get anywhere with you, can I?" Sterling rubbed his forehead. "But you took me by surprise, dammit. What would have been proper—less spectacular for you, maybe, but proper—was for you to contact me first. Let me know what you wanted to do. We could have worked something out."

"Could we? I didn't think so. What did you just say about

fellow spirits? Anyway, people did think we were working together. You weren't embarrassed—at least not in the way you
think."

"It's still a question of courtesy, Arcad, which you didn't
show. I am your host. I think you owe me."

Arcad spread his hands. "I'll accept that."

The concession relaxed Sterling enough so he could sit down
again. "Tell me. How much do you know about the history
of conjuring? You know, the lives of the late greats, their technique and philosophy."

"Not much, really."

"Well, that's something like my hobby. There's a lot to be
learned from some of these people, and it isn't limited to performing, either. One thing that seems to run as far back as
the records go is that a performer has to fight for the stage."

"How?"

"Think about sitting in a theater before showtime. That
empty stage is like a magnet, drawing the attention. It becomes
a possession—you could even see it at the party last night,
how everyone kept looking at the platform, not staring, understand, but checking, the way you'd check to see if your coat
was still on the hook at a cheap restaurant. When you come
onstage, you have to overcome a certain resentment. You're
an intruder, invading private property. What you have to do
is take command. Either with your looks, or your movements,
or your voice. You've got to show you mean business, that
you've got a right to be there. Then you can make your audience feel as if they're being let in on something special. That's
the hardest part. Once they surrender, they will allow themselves to be led. Manipulated. Fooled. That's why they're sitting there. But you have to get over that threshold. You've
got that ability, Arcad, I could tell that as soon as you stepped
up. I had to surrender that stage to you."

"That's very flattering—"

"I'm not finished. Next comes the mechanical part, the craft
of misdirection. Without the control, it's useless, but if a per-

former's got that first thing he can get by with secondary skills. When the two go together, you've got a genius. There've been people who could hang their meat out their fly and no one would notice because of what's going on in their hands. I like to think I'm as good as that. As for you—"

"I do lack experience."

"I'm not sure I believe that. You came up with a couple of oldies last night. I can see the bullet catch: Three-on-two switch, right? You steal a marked bullet and spit it out after the blank is shot. But the box. I was watching you. Over and over I thought, I know this trick! I've done it myself. *But you didn't make any of the moves!* I couldn't sleep last night trying to figure out how you did it. First I thought you might have planted boxes all over, in all the likely spots. But no one saw you before the party. And anyway, that pistol is a collector's item. There's not a bushel of 'em laying around. So you couldn't have buried the box beforehand, unless you're incredibly lucky." Sterling smiled a tight smile. "Then I thought you'd gotten to Russ."

"You questioned him?"

"I grilled his ass. Aside from whether or not he helped you with a practical joke, he's my security, you understand."

"Of course. I hope I haven't . . . inconvenienced him."

"He'll recover. But the end line is, I can't figure it. So why don't you open up. As one professional to another."

Arcad now laughed openly.

"What's so funny?"

"You. You're so serious about it." He paused, hoping Sterling would blurt out the information Nukhulls wanted. But the illusionist only frowned.

"There really isn't much to tell, Mr. Sterling."

"Try me."

"All right. I'll tell you a little story. There's a book I read once that's by a British woman who traveled to Tibet in order to become a Buddhist adept. She relates a very interesting concept taken from a sort of country parable. See, Tibet is really mountainous, and travel from village to village is difficult enough as it is. At that altitude, with afternoon light playing hell with the shadows, it's sometimes difficult to see things clearly. Once a traveler lost his hat along a trail. It got stuck in a bush, and the following day an ignorant peasant caught a glimpse of it as he rounded an outcropping of rock. The light was bad, and he didn't expect to see anything out of the ordinary, so naturally he became frightened and ran all the way to the next village with tales of a demon on the trail.

"Some were skeptical, but when others went near that bush and saw the hat moving in the wind, they became frightened too. They elaborated on what they saw, to justify their fright. A hat became a leathery face with red eyes. Then came reports of people being hounded by this new demon. Finally the villagers were forced to organize travel convoys, because everyone was too frightened to go alone."

Sterling stared straight ahead, lips pursed. There was something—shock?—which had drained some of the color from his face. Arcad wondered if he had indeed touched a nerve.

"My point is, the first man saw a hat and made it something more. The other men saw . . . well, saw what they wanted to see. A demon had been created. Whether or not there 'really' was a demon made absolutely no difference to those who believed in it."

Sighing, Sterling brought the tips of his fingers together. "So, what are you trying to tell me?"

"Mr. Sterling, I am not a legitimate performer. That's all I'm going to say."

"I see. . . . But you wanted to show me what you could do."

"I thought perhaps we could consult each other, or that I could assist you, or work for you." Arcad decided it was time for a small risk. He stood up. "I can see, though, that I presumed too much. I'll leave. Perhaps if someone could run me to Pacifica, so I can catch a hopper . . ."

It seemed to take Sterling a few moments to gain his bearings. Frowning again, he pushed his chair back from his desk and stood up.

"Arcad, you've come at an awkward time for me. But I'd like you to consider staying on for a few days. Let's get to know each other. After that, we'll see."

"I don't want to interrupt any projects—"

"Please." The word was spoken with extreme seriousness.

"Okay. I'll stay for as long as I don't get in your way. If I do, tell me."

Just then Kam opened the door and looked in.

"Oh, Kam, good, I was just going to call for you. Arcad here will be staying for a while. See if you can get him something to wear besides that undertaker's getup, will you?"

"Really! Let me take him from you, then."

"Do that. I've got to finish this by tonight." With that, Sterling returned to his papers. Whatever effect Arcad might have had on him seemed to have vanished. Wasting no time, Kam grabbed Arcad's arm and practically pulled him back to the elevator. Only when the MAGAZINE door closed behind them did she say anything.

"Oh, you handled him perfectly! I couldn't have done better myself."

"So you were listening."

"Arcad, you're a treasure!" She held his shoulders and gave him a quick kiss on the cheek. This he hadn't expected; his face got a little red.

"What's that for?"

"We've been needing someone like you around here for quite some time."

"You realize that I upset your husband again."

"Of course." She was looking at Arcad but not seeing him. Her mind was on other things, and it was working quickly.

"And you approve?"

"Al needs to be shown . . . occasionally . . . that great men can't be that way constantly."

"I don't really think I did that."

"But you stopped him! Al wanted to find you out. That way, he'd be able to deal with you in his usual combination of charm, flattery, and threats. He prides himself on being able to control people, and he couldn't get to you. That doesn't do him any harm, let me tell you."

As the car reached the third floor, Arcad decided to probe the husband-wife relationship a little. "Does he get to you, Mrs. Sterling?"

She stopped smiling. "Once I could honestly answer no to that question. Now—well, let's say he knows the territory. Maybe I need you to show me what I'm doing wrong."

"That's asking a little too much from someone you've just met, don't you think?"

"You're turning me down."

"Look. I don't want to sound too cryptic, but there are things about me—well, things that it wouldn't do you any good to know."

Suddenly she was angry. "My husband prides himself on being mysterious. It's his life. But I'm damn sick and tired of it!"

"I'm sorry," he said firmly, hoping the matter would be closed. His elation had folded. All he'd done was not make any of the moves Sterling expected. The illusionist had been thrown off—but Arcad was still short of success. His expression must have looked gray, because suddenly Kam brightened and touched his shoulder.

"Aw, never mind. Listen, I do have to get to the market. Ring Russ if you want any lunch. Dinner will be at seven or so. Until then, amuse yourself as you like. There're books, the video. Oh, but please stay out of the magazine. Al is very touchy about it—you know, private retreat and all."

"All right. Thanks."

She turned and walked briskly away; Arcad knew that whatever she had started between them was far from over.

5.

It was a cold night at the Santa Cruz Compound, where Bruce Nukhulls had returned to prepare a summary report that was to be forwarded directly to President Houseman. All the information had previously been communicated in one form or another to the president. Nevertheless, because Nukhulls' staff in Washington suspected that the old man was wavering, Nukhulls thought it wise to give Houseman an easy reference that could double as an in-conference weapon should the need arise. Really, with the disorganized state of the capital, it wasn't surprising that so many regions harbored the sentiments that were openly expressed in the West. The Confederal Union was so nominal as it was, with each of the seventeen regions begrudging their assessed portion of the Confederal budget more and more each year, that the whole structure might well collapse without a war. For that reason, there were more than western interests at stake here, and Nukhulls wanted to be sure that everyone back East in a position to aid his project understood it very well.

2/26/79
Lenore Houseman
Nukhulls Add: Orig SC Comp WR
Eyes Only

1. EM-WAVE TESTING SERIES LANGLEY NOW COMPLETE, SUMMARY REPORT ENCLOSURE

Results indicate that waves of escalating frequency have predicted effects within a margin of $\pm.076$, a significant value sufficient to justify the procedure in the July 2079 broadcast. I consider this particular broadcast prime target for the following reasons: a) emotional camouflage provided by the participation of Alphonse Sterling; b) the potentially large audience available on that date, particularly in the Western Region, due to Sterling's popular following here; c) the already patriotic overtones of the July Fourth celebration, which leaves viewers more open to manipulation in this vein.

The appendix to this report confirms that a video rider signal adequate for close-effect wave generation off home video sets is effective within a proximity radius of three meters. Projections of 69% effectiveness for those within that distance give us 43% of adult population in WR, or approximately 6 million adults with moderate to strong reaction to wave/image sequence proposed. Demographically, this number will be sufficient to sway the political considerations behind any move of WR toward secession. Naturally, all is dependent upon WR agreeing to accept continental broadcast feed. However, in view of Sterling's already announced plans, such an agreement will most certainly be forthcoming.

2. ANALYSIS OF ILLUSION WITH REGARD TO WAVE/IMAGE SEQUENCE

At this point we do not know the exact nature of Sterling's proposed illusion. However, a comparative analysis of some twenty-five such events in the past reveals this common progression:

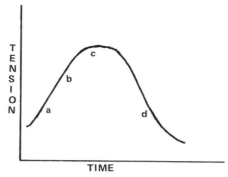

a) establishing of condition of imminent peril, with performer clearly separate from those conditions
b) willing submission on part of performer to such conditions
c) resulting interval of uncertainty, leading to:
d) shattering of tension as peril is overcome by performer

As plotted on fig. 1., optimum area for insertion of message lies between c & d on the down curve. Physiological effects of the strong Em pulse can be successfully masked by the overt tension generated by the illusion in progress. The message/impression inserted at this point will be left to your discretion; however, I strongly suggest a theme of unity and security deriving from the continuation of the central government. Perhaps you may include your own name as well, counterimposed to the anxiety previously experienced by the viewing audience. Fig. 2. in appendix indicates the exact signal strength, pulse length, and frequency which will produce the optimum results, regardless of message semantics.

3. STERLING AS FACTOR

Here I am forced to speculate. There has been some conjecture as to the reliability of Alphonse Sterling as instrument to wave/pulse sequence. Naturally, because of his personal relationship with Peter Deliewe and some of the other leading figures in the political structure of the WR, it is not feasible to directly request his assistance for the procedure. As of this moment he has not outlined the exact nature or form of the illusion he will perform, though I am confident it will follow the general configuration described in fig. 1. We are aware that it will be performed in earth orbit.

My own staff has expressed suspicion that Sterling might have motives of his own in agreeing to perform during a celebration which is being actively opposed by most WR leaders. Though I personally doubt that Sterling will open appeal for secession before a national audience, there are a number of things he might do which would interfere, either directly or indirectly, with our operation. Accordingly, I have placed agent RA in the field, with the aim of firming up our advance information. His report will be forthcoming; in any event, success is statistically indicated, whatever Sterling might do, *so long as he performs an illusion.* At this point we have no indication that he will do otherwise.

To reunion. My greetings to Mrs. Houseman, with the hope that she is recovering well from her stroke.

Nukhulls

Nukhulls looked at the memo with loathing. It was bad enough that he was required to produce such reports at regular intervals, but the fact that his plans might be overthrown by the doddering Houseman infuriated him. God only knew what kept the president from the edge of senility. He'd been old when elected in '52, swept in on the wave of reaction to the enervating quarter century spent in the systematic destruction of mainland China. Just five years later, Houseman had been forced to issue the depopulation order "for the greater good," looking the other way as the military technicians went to work again. The results of that decision should have been enough to kill him, but again Houseman hung on, right through Continental Convention in the '60s and the subsequent dismantling of federal power.

That, he was still trying to bring back. Nukhulls remembered the mawkish speech made on the eve of the Tricentennial, two years before. It was a speech that brought tears to many eyes—but no political results whatsoever. The regions still mouthed their threats, and in the West the situation had come to the point of total separation. The distance between D.C. and San Metro were simply too great, with nowhere near enough mutual interests to cement any bonds firmly.

But Houseman still tried, proclaiming unwavering devotion to principles that no longer made any sense. He was a fool. Let someone younger take over, a woman perhaps, someone with some brains, for all the difference it would make.

Politics bored Nukhulls. His interest in this matter was purely scientific. And artistic, or so he allowed himself to admit. Wearily he looked at his portable viewing screen. A dragon—the same image used by the Chinese in their subliminal terror strike preceding the first tactical attack on Washington—glowed in reds and greens. Perhaps he should send a copy of that along with his report, so Houseman could see what he'd be using—if Houseman could still see.

Someone knocked at his door.

"Come."

"Evening, sir." It was Kelley, with the Metro newspaper. Nukhulls waved his hand without looking at him.

"Throw it on the bed, will you, Kelley?"

"Sir, there's someone here to see you."

"Well, send him away, dammit, I'm working."

"It's Senator Duenos."

"Christ." Nukhulls sighed, rising stiffly, memo in hand. "All right. Get this out, will you?" Kelley saluted and disappeared into the night. Ah, well, maybe Duenos was just what he needed at the moment to break his lethargy.

"Bruce!" The senator charged into the room. "Burning the midnight oil, I see."

"Senator, come on in." Nukhulls watched the overweight politician settle heavily onto his bed. "What can I do for you?"

"Let me catch my breath first. I'm exhausted! I'll have to spend the night on the compound, I'm afraid."

"It is your home."

Duenos grinned. "Officially."

"Of course."

"Whew. That's better. I've just come from a four-hour meeting of the Regional Planning Commission."

"Can I interest you in some coffee?"

"Anything!"

Nukhulls rinsed a cup in the sink. "One of their public sessions, eh?" he asked, handing the steaming cup to a grateful Duenos.

"Thanks. Yes; you don't think they'd do their scheming in the presence of a Confederal representative, do you? But I go. They appreciate these things back East, even though it's usually a waste of time. Water release into the Sacramento delta. Airport maintenance assistance for LAX. A godawful bore."

In order to cut off any elaboration, Nukhulls anticipated him. "But tonight was different."

"Mm. You could fuel hoppers on this stuff."

"Talk to your staff."

"You can see why I don't live here. Anyway, tonight I was damn near asleep when all of a sudden Tom Stassen—he's the commissioner from down Fresno way who's what they call a separatist—brought up something that wasn't on the agenda. Get this. He wanted a policy statement on network hook-ups for political broadcasts. You should have seen Deliewe's face! Those two have never gotten along very well, you know. They don't go for Deliewe's kind of fence-straddling down in the valley. But he managed to control himself, and made this pompous statement about how that was a matter that would be dealt with directly by his own office. Then he tried to go on to other business, but Stassen kept the floor and had a statement read into the record outlining his district's total opposition to any broadcast, regardless of content. Then he finished off by commenting that he wished to know once and for all what the governor was doing about his promises to obtain autonomy for the region."

"You were awake by this time?"

"Just listen. Deliewe knows how to chair a meeting. He said that as the matter had not yet been decided, a number of opinions might prove valuable. So he turns to me and says, 'Senator, for the record also, what are your feelings concerning this matter?' "

"Which sparked the oratory flames, no doubt."

Duenos lay back on the bed. "In modest fashion."

"So? What did you tell them?"

"I gave them the modified unity-speech number three. You know, common history, mutual cooperation for the interests of both, new situation makes it necessary to reassess relationships, bla bla woof woof. Then I added that I couldn't see how a few hours of entertainment, mixed with a little maudlin history, could possibly affect the political destiny of a region with so obviously bright a future. Naturally, Stassen wanted no part of that—but Deliewe gaveled him down and stated that he found very little he disagreed with. On to other business."

Nukhulls scratched his head. "That's interesting, Jack, very interesting. What did you make of it?"

"I think something's in the wind. I've understood Deliewe himself in the past to be opposed to political broadcasts. I think something's changed his mind."

Nukhulls was grateful for this intelligence. But he did not want to get Duenos involved too deeply. Not only because he was unsure of the senator's true feelings on the subject of secession—but also because of Duenos' limited ability to keep anything quiet.

"Maybe so. Sterling might have had a word with him about it at the party the other night. He only signed the contract three weeks ago. But speaking of the party, did you see that guy get up there—"

"Bruce," Duenos said, getting up, "I'll save you the trouble of leading me on. I simply came to report like a good public servant." He noticed the dragon image on the screen. "A bit grim, isn't it?"

"I—"

"Oh, never mind. I'm going up the hill to try and get some sleep. Thanks for the coffee."

"Thank *you.*"

"Glad to be of help. Listen, I wish you'd be careful. Whatever you're planning around Sterling, keep in mind that he's very, very smart. And tough."

"I will."

"I hope your boy out there knows that too. Well, good night."

After the senator had gone, Nukhulls considered this latest bit of information. The fact that Deliewe had changed his mind concerning the broadcasts seemed to confirm Nukhulls' suspicions that Sterling might be planning something more than an illusion for the Fourth. He looked down at his notes analyzing Sterling's performances and pondered the consequences of those suspicions.

Sterling's ability to control his audience was already formidable: What if he really had developed psychokinetic powers? What if instead of merely sensing a peak of tension, he could actually produce it at will? Given the man's egotistic temperament, there was no telling what he might attempt. Arcad, at least, was basically a shy person with a highly developed, sometimes paralyzing ethical sense. And even with Arcad, Nukhulls did not feel entirely safe.

He struggled to escape the profound depression that was steadily settling down on him. Compared to what Arcad or Sterling could do, his own efforts seemed so heavy-handed. He remembered the first successful test of an Em-wave generator some six years ago:

The room full of paid volunteers, half of them doe-eyed students, the other half scraped from the tokay-lacquered gutters of D.C. The movie of a little boy playing with a puppy. The clumsy, mushroom-shaped broadcast coil behind the screen, throwing off a theta pulse of two cps in synch with the 1:1200 image of two wolves fighting, tearing at each other. He'd felt such elation at the screaming reaction! People scared out of their minds without knowing why. How confident he'd been then of this vehicle for his own control.

He had been confident enough to let Arcad go, even though his process was far from refined, far from being able to do what he wanted it to do.

And now, even though it was. . . . He glanced down at his newspaper. Argentine troops were barely holding their own along the Río de la Plata, despite heavy losses to the other side. What idiots these politicians were, clinging to the old ways when the alternatives were there. Bodies, it was always bodies to be redistributed, without a thought given to the brain. Desires could be restructured painlessly, with social aims achieved at a fraction of the old costs. Nukhulls knew that with the proper equipment, he'd have the war ended in a half hour in favor of whatever side was employing him. Erase the concept of Mother Brazil. Kick Father Argentina out! They were no longer necessary.

I wonder if I am, he thought. He decided to get another hour's work completed before going to sleep.

He flashed a slide of Houdini stepping inside a large metal cannister filled with water. Here the audience was still not quite convinced that the performer was really going to go through with being locked inside. Let them think about it: a beta pulse between 13 and 30 cps would help. Now the developing image should be just barely perceptible, perhaps 1:1500 of the eyes only, say.

Angrily he turned off the projector. It was all too arbitrary, too piecemeal. He'd never be certain if the thing was correct until it was actually tried. If only he could get Arcad to stand on a mountain and simply broadcast compulsion, throw the moon out of orbit, turn the sun purple!

That, however, was impossible. Nukhulls had made it that way by programming Arcad's mother into him.

Mother's dead, you killed her
Mother's dead, you killed her
Mother's dead, *you* killed her.

By limiting the psychokinetic with guilt, Nukhulls had kept a hand on him. Arcad was in constant horror of something he had not done. Perhaps the answer was to release him and forget all the rest.

Maybe later, Nukhulls thought, turning out the light.

6.

Fighting a ten-knot breeze that blew in salty from the ocean, Arcad struggled to reach the top of the long grade known as Devil's Slide. Despite the winter dampness, which he could feel through his borrowed jacket, the exertion kept him from feeling too cold. He halted at the base of Houdini's rock to survey the distance traveled from the beach, perhaps two kilometers away, where sand blanketed the remains of California's Route 1. Misted by the wind, shale cliffs glistened. All very beautiful, all very lonely, much more so than the overgrown residential streets of Diablo, less than eighty kilometers away.

He could have been on another planet, such were the changes imposed upon him in the last week.

It's what I deserve, he thought. First, for not figuring that Nukhulls would have planted that Finder on me. Second, for not refusing to help him.

Errors of omission, which had allowed Nukhulls to appeal successfully to Arcad's sense of duty. Arcad had a job to complete. It was time to get to work, no matter how much he wanted to stay out of whatever was going on between Kam and her husband. Arcad was forced to admit that Kam's behavior baffled him so far. There was quite definitely an attraction between them, and yet she was blatant in her manipulations too, so blatant that he was afraid he was going to have to alter her feelings, much as he hated doing it. But he loved it too, and that's what made her interference so impossible.

Do your job, it's all that matters.

He finally reached the hopper pad, which looked larger in the daylight, where he noticed a path worn into the brush across the saddle of rock. It led to a concrete loading dock secured by a corrugated rolling door. Another entrance to the third level; interesting. A garage, perhaps, with a hopper and a few motorcycles, and a doorway through that to Sterling's precious MAGAZINE. Arcad considered: Of course he could get the door open, but it would take a few moments, and he didn't want to be seen. Much simpler to gain access from the inside.

So, he mounted the concrete stairway. Overhead, cormorants screamed around the hazed solar disk, mocking him. Jesus. Nukhulls thought it was all so easy, and it might have been, without having *her* to think about. Somehow, Kam was on to him. Maybe she didn't know what he was or exactly what his mission entailed, but she had sensed that he was there to challenge her husband. She seemed the type of person who in a fight would use any weapon at her disposal. And if that weapon was a tall, silver-haired stranger, so what? Perhaps he'd be just what she needed to "get to" Alphonse Sterling, as she'd put it earlier in the day. As for her own plans, who could tell? Nothing specific, maybe, except a wish to get a changing relationship back to an outmoded equilibrium. It was ridiculous.

All you have to do is make her stop.

But I haven't the right to interfere.

You do if she keeps you from doing your job.

The job is to be done with finesse. When I'm gone, no one should be able to tell I've been here.

Trying to shake off his confusion, Arcad reached the landing and used the key Kam had given him to gain entry. He walked into the large room where the party had been held the previous evening. Everything had been cleaned up and the stage was empty and without lights. Behind it, the drapes were open to a picture window that spanned the width of the room. The glass was a little dirty. Arcad thought it was probably a struggle keeping it clean, what with constant fog and wind—along with the smoke generated at numerous parties. To the left of the window, through the doorway leading to the kitchen, Arcad found a stairway. He decided to check with Kam about dinner, and perhaps, with a bit of deft questioning, find out where she'd be for the next hour or so. Sterling was probably still downstairs.

But at the top of the staircase he heard their voices:

"No, I don't understand at all!"

"Maybe if you shut your yap for once you would."

"Look, Al, you know better than I do, as soon as you lose contact with your audience you've made the job twice as hard. On video, in orbit—impossible. Nobody's going to buy it."

"I think they will."

"What makes you so sure? You're only as good as our last show, remember that. This thing is stupid!"

"Kam, you're going to have to trust me on this one."

"Trust you! How the hell can I trust you, locked away in that damned room every day, and now you're going against every single thing we've learned together."

"Maybe I've got something new."

"Like what?"

"Like I told you. It's not ready yet; you're going to have to wait. When the time's right, you'll know."

"I'm sick of it. This is your wife, remember?"

"Then start acting like one and mind your own fucking business!"

A door slammed far down the hallway. There was silence, then rapid footsteps—Sterling's, Arcad guessed—followed by the sound of running water. Arcad listened carefully for the elevator. It wasn't being used. He had his chance. He went back down and saw where the stairway continued to the lower level. Something about that argument made him feel very

70

strange, as if he had been shaken loose from his own place in the world. Somehow, when Nukhulls had told him that Sterling might have powers similar to his own, it had all been clinical, necessary information. Not once had Arcad considered what it might mean.

It meant that he might not be alone anymore. That was something he'd accepted years ago, when he learned to tuck the emotions away where they couldn't interfere with the day-to-day business of living. And now they all started coming back, the longing, the loneliness. The guilt—

You have your job, Arcad, get on with it. Forget her, forget him. Follow a procedure and get the hell out.

He was at the MAGAZINE door again, opposite the elevator door. He began pushing through—

There was a hand on his shoulder.

"Where do you think you're going, pal?" It was Russ. Arcad had not realized the size of the man before: he was at least as tall, and over twenty-three kilograms heavier. And he was doing his job, which was, at the moment, to provide effective security, charged with an element of revenge. Arcad regretted what he had to do nevertheless. The technique was something like turning a key in a lock, with the front part of the brain.

"I'm upstairs sleeping comfortably. Find out, please, how soon I should be awakened for dinner."

Rusty's expression did not change. He simply turned, got into the elevator, and rode away. Good. Very, very good.

Goddamn Nukhulls!

Arcad went into the MAGAZINE proper and chose first to look around Sterling's office. The desk was in the same littered condition in which Arcad had seen it earlier in the day. The pipe, with a few ashes scattered near it, lay atop a legal pad scrawled with calculations pertaining to "payload 900 tns. metrc." Arcad flipped through the pages and found nothing else. Beneath the pad, however, was an appointment calendar. There was a notation, "meeting with Plnng Commis.," listed for sometime the next day. Later in the week, Sterling intended to "see Kaiser per fabrication costs," with a reminder in red to "stress advertis. potential for possible reduction."

There were other papers, which seemed to be notes for an autobiographical article Sterling apparently was working on: interesting, but not quite to the point. Arcad started on the desk drawers, finding decks of cards, paper clips stuck to a lodestone, a few silks, financial records, bits of knotted cord, a carved ivory ball-within-a-ball. There were also pencil erasers and gold needles strung through a thread. A nice mix of the mundane and the borderline fantastic.

In the middle drawer Arcad found something a little more curious. It was a little model of something like a boom balanced on a steep pyramid of dark plastic. Arcad set it upright on its base and turned on the desk lamp in order to see it a little better. The structure rocked on its pivot. It was similar in design to the cranes one saw atop buildings under construction, and in fact it did have a counterweight on one end. At the opposite end, however, instead of pulleys and line tackle there was a strange arrangement: First, what looked like a tiny cage. Attached to this, a fairing which supported twin paddles wound with fine copper wire. Between them was suspended a gleaming ball bearing. The boom terminated with another fairing, which led to another, even tinier cage. A single thread of monofilament plastic ran from the first cage, through the ball bearing, and into the other. Arcad gave the weighted end a push with his thumb, watching as the thing revolved in wobbly fashion about the pivot. He picked it up and saw PASSAGE THROUGH MOLTEN SILVER etched to one side of the base.

He formed no conclusions, and, on impulse, he decided to pocket it. He closed the drawers, satisfied himself that everything was arranged pretty much the way he'd found it, then switched off the light. Nothing really added up to much. Arcad decided to try the padlocked museum, more out of curiosity than any hope of finding the exact answers he sought.

In front of the other door he reached for the lock. It was old and very heavy. Perhaps it had some value as an antique;

he decided against melting it away. Arcad tried visualizing the mechanism, lining up the pins and drivers one by one so he could turn the plug in the cylinder without a key. He tried once, was forced to try again—two of the springs had been deliberately weakened! Finally, though, the lock popped open. Deciding not to trouble with locking it behind him, Arcad went in. He caught sight of a rheostat and brought up the lights.

The room was all wrong, partitioned with panels whose angles were impossibly acute; space seemed to shrink and grow whenever some new reference rearranged the impression gained the instant before. The true proportions of wall, ceiling, and floor were hidden by soft folds of deep velvet draperies. But there was a pathway—indicated by a glowing line painted on the floor—which spiraled in toward the center. The six tall bookshelves immediately in front of him blocked any view of these inner displays. Arcad gave the collection a cursory examination. Most of the volumes were old, some leather-bound, nearly all of them concerned with the conjurer's trade: *Fifty Years in the Magic Circle,* by Signor Blitz; *The Life and Times of the Compte de Paris.* The collection seemed comprehensive enough, though Arcad lacked enough background in the subject to be really certain.

Oh, it was indecent, this going through another man's things. No doubt Sterling might have invited him down here for a guided tour later in the day. Still, the glamour of some of this stuff might have been dulled by an Alphonse Sterling narration. Arcad followed the painted line inward. In the red light were shapes of heavy wood and gleaming metal, which Arcad was unable to identify, but some he could: false-bottomed cabinets, covered in molting plush, decorated in faded heavens of lamé moons and brocade stars. Side tables, complete with net servantes or black-art wells (both useful for vanishing small objects) stood cold in chipping marble. Bamboo cages, sliding mirrors in cracked walnut frames—all had an appearance of utility, and the only utility was deception.

Inward, inward. Four dummies sat on a small table. Arcad

pinged a turbaned metal sage on its nose. There was a whir of gears as the automaton perused a set of cards mounted before it; a jack was selected and offered to the intruder.

"Sorry, old boy. I was thinking three of clubs."

It snatched the card away with its perpetual leer, returning to spring-stopped inertia. Arcad smiled and went on past a wire gooseneck, used in levitation acts, to where the painted line was cut off by another doorway. More velvet, hung from the ceiling, covered a wall of plywood which protected an area perhaps fifteen meters in diameter. There was a small sign on the door:

Ehrich Weiss Collection.

Arcad closed his eyes, preparing to open that one too.

"Go ahead. I'd like to see how you do it."

He jumped before he recognized the voice. Kam laughed at his discomfiture and leveled a hand crystal at him.

"Don't look so dismayed, darling. It's my suspicious nature. Rusty kept insisting you were in your room asleep—though I'd just been in there, and no you." She fingered her weapon slowly, as though it were made of soft, warm gold, feeling, apparently, that her moment of success was at hand. And, keeping with the feral pose, she decided to play with her victim before consuming him. Playing the part, Arcad affected nervous embarrassment.

"I'm slightly too curious for my own good, I suppose."

"You choose to pry at the first opportunity. Which leads me to suspect that your concern is more than personal. Tell me, how did you get that lock open?"

"It's just a trick I know."

"The same one that was going to get you in there."

Arcad said nothing; instead, he watched the triumph in the way she leaned against a brass prop stand. She was trying to make him very conscious of the mercy she could bestow. Too conscious. Arcad realized that the point at which he could

74

safely divert her had passed. He must wait, however, until she committed herself.

"You don't have anything to say? Perhaps that's just as well." She licked her lips slowly. "You know, Arcad, I knew it wasn't true when you said you couldn't help me. Right now I've got the distinct feeling that you were sent here. I think I could solve all my problems simply by putting a hole right in the middle of your forehead. I'll tell Al you're a Confederal spy. That should make him angry enough to cancel his illusion. Perhaps he'll be more inclined to take me into his confidence. Then again, I might not have to be so drastic. Why don't you tell me what it is you want, and we'll see."

"Unfortunately, that's none of your business."

"Did I add that Al and the sheriff here are old friends?"

"No." Arcad froze her for a moment, and she stood with her eyes glazed. He had her open her hand, took the crystal and pocketed it, then released her. The color had gone from her face as she blinked her eyes. It was Arcad's turn to smile.

"You were saying?"

"How—"

"The hand is quicker than the eye, my dear Mrs. Sterling." He watched her sag with an expression like that of a bride locked out of the bedroom on her honeymoon night. It was difficult not to laugh at her.

"Since I seem to have surprised you, I'll admit that, yes, I am a spy. I'd like to get inside this room, if you happen to have a key. . . ."

Kam recovered a little. "No one has it but Al. He's the only one who ever goes inside."

"All right. Who's Ehrich Weiss?"

"That's the original Houdini's real name. Al has a lot of his old stage props, and . . ."

"And what?"

She made a move toward him, her eyes glistening. When Arcad stepped aside she actually looked hurt. Arcad felt his determination beginning to give way.

"He spends all his evenings in there. Stays for hours. When he comes back to me he's got a look on his face—he's not the same person! Something changes him. . . . Jesus, Arcad, you've got to help me!"

"How long has this been going on?"

"Five months, six months," she replied sharply. "Who knows! Ever since he's been doing it, he doesn't care a thing about our act. No more bookings, no new illusions—if you only knew how much time we used to spend planning things, working out drawings, stage diagrams. Now it's all his last big trick, he says. Passage through molten silver he calls it. It's something that can't possibly work—"

Arcad remembered the model in his pocket. "He's explained the trick to you?"

"Yes, but it makes absolutely no sense. He doesn't have a way out this time. It's not an illusion, it's a vehicle for something else, and that he refuses to discuss. Oh, Arcad—"

She got her arms around his neck before he could push her gently, reluctantly away. Something was draining him now, keeping him from thinking things out properly. In the red light, with the honey smell of her hair, and the scratches on his neck from her nails, it was impossible to sort out his impressions. She was going to have her way, weapon or no.

"Mrs. Sterling," he said, "it seems we are both concerned about your husband. Perhaps if you help me I might be able to do the same for you."

She immediately abandoned her emotional pose. "Go on."

"Do you have any idea where his written plans for the illusion might be?"

"There aren't any. I'm the one who draws up plans. More than likely it's all in his head."

"Can you get him to talk?"

She smiled ruefully. "My success with men seems limited lately. Wait a minute, though. Can you fly a hopper?"

"Barely."

"Good. If you'll agree to chauffeur me tomorrow, you may

be able to see what you've been after."

Arcad looked at her. "I don't want to seem rude, but when someone's held a crystal my way I tend to remain slightly suspicious. Tell me how and what."

"We've got a warehouse in San Metro down by the old Civic Center. Al's got a meeting scheduled there tomorrow with some of his friends in the regional government. I think he'll be giving them the word about his plans. I'm supposed to go with him to help work the demonstration—that much he still needs me for. I can tell him I'm going in early from Pacifica. Meanwhile, we'll ferry up and make a few preparations of our own when we get there. Then you may hide yourself to watch the proceedings. They ought to be interesting, at the very least. What do you say?"

"All right."

"You *are* a treasure!"

"There's one thing, however—"

"I have trouble keeping track of conditions."

"A simple caution only."

"Which is?"

"I've lived alone for a few years now. You might say that my present assignment constitutes a return from retirement. In that time I've become accustomed to dealing with an unimpeachable character—"

"Who is?" she broke in coldly.

"Myself. Let's cut the demonstrations. I'm insisting on honesty from you so we can both know where we stand. I don't want to get to the center and find out it's on the end of a string."

"I could have given you the same speech."

"It wouldn't have meant as much."

"Fair enough." She came toward him again. "Let's seal this bargain nobly, shall we?" This time he could not resist her kiss. Her lips worked softly over his, with a touch of her tongue, and it was she who pulled away, just as he began to respond.

"You're an attractive man, Arcad. Tell me your first name."

"It's Ryan. . . ."

Kam kissed him again. "I think I prefer Arcad. You're not much like a Ryan. Mmm."

"Your husband wouldn't appreciate finding us here," he offered weakly. For a moment he considered taking the warmth out of her, but it had been so long since he'd held a woman in this way. . . .

At any rate, to resist was his own concern. She sighed and agreed with him.

"You're right. Dinner's ready anyway. But you may see me later this evening. If you want."

"I thought we discussed demonstrations."

She brushed his lips with her fingers. "And this falls under that category?"

Perhaps it was a mistake, but he left the question unanswered.

7.

As a demented priest on a hot night throws his blankets off and prays for the succubus to come, Ryan Arcad was unable to get much sleep that night. Just a few feet away, Kam slept next to a man who had become a stranger to her. Yet, she still stretched her body in the darkness, arching her back, with a small cry, her breasts flattened above the extended line of her neck, her hair brushing the soft skin between her shoulders. With her mouth open, moonlight would just touch her front teeth and the glistening tip of her tongue.

Yet, she did not come. Arcad wondered if he was responsible, perhaps erasing her desire by reflex. Then again, she might be motivating him in spite of her promise. He wanted to call her with his mind, bring her to him. . . .

But that would be the same as keeping her away. He had to let it be; there might be another chance later. Arcad thought about the dinner, which had to be considered a social success. Sterling had been effusive and full of energy, Kam his blushing foil. For the pleasure of them both, he had performed some close-in table magic. Sterling was good with sleights, mixing his moves so well that no matter how Arcad had concentrated on following the bit of crumpled napkin, it always seemed to appear from a spot he hadn't suspected. Arcad tried his hand too, multiplying kernels of corn with his own special method, successfully baffling both Kam and Sterling. As before, he'd made none of the proper moves—yet, so light was the tone of the meeting that Sterling appeared content to let the mystery pass. Arcad got the feeling that all of them were waiting for something to happen, waiting for him to initiate the action.

> The Succubus on wings of Night
> Her Victim doth attend . . .

Arcad was only reminded of what he considered the core of his problem: To survive with an ability to do everything, he was constantly forced to cheat himself of things that might have happened without his interference. One changed too much in order to avoid having to change everything, and thus skirted the touch of minds which provides the only spark of interest in a human life. The result was that Arcad forced himself to protect an order he could not directly experience.

> With movement soft and secret plan
> She doth negate the Will of Man

To experience that order would leave him a choice: if the order is correct, then I am its instrument and must correct all deviations.

> Sore Pleasure's heat masks her Deceit

If the order is not correct, then it would have to be changed, and Arcad had decided early in his life, after the death of his mother, that he was not God, never could be God

> 'Til widespread aim fans Demon's flame
> and *dam'd* without Amend.

No matter what might happen.

For that reason he had allowed himself to be used. Mission became chore; strength of mind became strength of back. Minds were changed like erratically worn cams, and whenever ethical difficulties arose, Nukhulls had been there to smooth them. Both men knew what Arcad needed to survive: an overwhelming pragmatism that Arcad sorely missed now. This time Nukhulls had tossed him loose. Why? He had said, "Look at him. Either Sterling's gone far ahead on technique—or he's like you." The meaning was just becoming apparent.

Arcad could no longer rely upon the old limits. He would have to redefine them in order to tackle something that was potentially bigger than he was. That was the essence of this particular mission, and if Arcad were successful, what then? Would Nukhulls be able to deal with the remains?

He forced himself to sleep until the alarm sounded. He pulled on his clothes and stumbled into the bathroom to splash water on his face. It felt like porcelain. Arcad wondered about Kam, and was about to go look for her when she slipped into his room. Her face was full, lips swollen with sleep, or perhaps not with sleep.

"Hi. Just up?"

"Yeah. What's going on?"

"Al's down working. I told him I'd be over at Grove Street by ten-thirty. The meeting's for twelve."

Arcad looked at her, surprised to discover that she at least approximated his night image. "He let you in on the big secret?"

"No. But you are supposed to be a little under the weather and sleeping it off. Let's see . . ." She pulled a couple of extra pillows from a closet shelf and brought them to the bed, arranging them beneath the covers to give approximately the appearance of someone lost to sprawling slumber.

"There. That ought to be enough to fool Rusty, seeing as how he was stupid enough to think you were sleeping all of yersterday. Anyway, I want to make sure you're placed far away from the scene of the crime."

"So there *is* going to be some of that."

"Espionage. Premeditated interference. I've decided, just for fun, to make my husband appear slightly less masterful than he might like. A failure today might influence his decision to go through with the Passage."

"What do you have in mind?"

"All in good time, my friend. Let's go."

They went outside and down the stairway, with Arcad wishing for a warmer coat because of the fog. At the base of the rock, Kam took a key and opened the corrugated door. Inside was a hopper and, as Arcad had suspected, another locked door to the museum. Kam grabbed the front gear T-bar herself and began pulling the machine out of the immediate dock area.

"Let me," Arcad offered.

"This is far enough. Al doesn't want a blast accident in the vicinity of his precious collection."

Arcad glanced at the dented foils of the hopper. The inductor scoops looked as if they'd each sucked half a ton of gravel. Kam laughed at his concern.

"Oh, it flies. Al usually takes the boat into San, though. I don't think he likes depending on such a small thing. Trapped with no escape and all."

"Okay." He got in, struggling to find some kind of comfortable position amid the collection of filthy rags and empty oil cans, and a battered toolbox which was no help at all in working the foot controls. Kam leaned over to give him a hand stowing things; finally, he sealed the bubble, hit the ignition button—and got no response.

"There's a glow plug in these old jobs—here." She pulled out a knob above the stick on the floor console. After a few seconds it turned red.

"Try it now."

Inductors vibrated, working up to an operational whine. Arcad held his breath, gave it the foot throttle, and pulled his stick. They were airborne.

"Not exactly an ace, are you?"

"Take a cab. What's the heading, anyway?"

"That's the wrong question to ask *me,* dear. But bring us over the fog—we should be able to see some buildings. Then try for a beam off the Alcatraz Beacon. It's early—shouldn't be too much traffic coming from up our way."

In the white-out, their machine responded sluggishly, as drops of moisture ran straight down from the apex of the bubble. Then, all at once, they popped into the blue.

"That's the one thing I don't like about the Slide, Arcad. You can count the sunny days on the fingers of one hand."

"Then you should pop up more often."

"I'd never want to come down. Got the beam?"

"Yup. I'll let it do the work for a while. Look at that!" The fog bank extended west and south all the way to the horizon. Inland, however, the warmer air over the land had driven away the mist, exposing winter-green hills all the way down the peninsula. Only at the Metro limits near the base of Mount San Bruno did it seem that the fog had its way again, covering the flat, fingerless hand of what had once been called San Francisco. But, just as Kam had said, a good dozen white-and-buff spires poked through the cloud cover at two hundred meters, giving the appearance of a small town in the clouds.

"It's easy to see how Sir Francis Drake sailed completely by. We should be okay, though. Alcatraz will loop us around the gate and into Marina Green." She pointed toward two rusty towers, one of which was twisted off center and tilted to the east.

"Look at it. That's what's left of the old bridge. Between there and where we are now is Ocean Beach. That was the scene of many a battle."

"How so?"

"During the days of the security perimeter. My father was captain of a beach battalion. He said refugees used to try to come in by the hundreds. Out in the surf were antipersonnel barriers, wire, drowning snares. The bodies floated like seaweed there, and still they tried. Later, the attempts were organized, like military landings. But the shore emplacements were always too much. Al told me that he and a couple of his friends from Chicago tried getting in that way once."

"And they didn't make it."

"Nope. His friends were killed. Al managed to come up with the raft and had to paddle all the way south to Half Moon Bay. That's when he decided to try the inland route. Hiked across the peninsula, crossed the mud flats to Newark, then over the Coast Range and north to Diablo—in the middle of summer! I guess he figured he could sneak in over the Caldecott Gate on the old tunnel road." She laughed.

"Stupid?"

"It was only the most fortified sector of the barrier! Ha, after eighteen years he still won't admit that the only reason he got in was me."

"You mean the Great Houdini couldn't get through a little charged wire?"

"Honey, when I first saw him he could barely get through an open door! I was your typical fifteen-year-old brat, what with Daddy on duty all the time, and Mom sort of drunk whenever he wasn't home. Who needed school? I got it into my head that a little jaunt into terrible, dangerous Diablo would be some kind of great fun. I should have been locked up, really, because twenty years ago it was rough out there—squatters' camps full of hungry refugees. Very little food. Less water. I was lucky to get out in one piece. But I had a smart mouth. Also a very sharp thirteen-centimeter dirk. Then there was my residency card. Anytime things got too bad, I could always waltz right home again."

"Which you did."

"Oh yes—babies get tired of the sandbox, you know. And in spite of my resourcefulness, I'd had some pretty bad scares. So, one day I decided to go back. Just out of Orinda, I saw this little guy staring at about two meters of wire outside a cow pasture. He was so intense about it! For about five minutes he stares, then he lets out a scream and a half and tries jumping it. Almost made it, too—just caught the bottom of his pants on the top strand, then *bam*, right onto his face! I couldn't help laughing, which wasn't too smart, because he could have been a hacker or something. As it was, he was pretty mad.

He called me some things I was still unfamiliar with, before I stalked up to him. 'Who the hell are you?' I scream. And then he looked at me with those blue eyes. 'Me?' he says. 'Me, I'm the Great Houdini.'" Kam sighed. "And I believed him. . . ."

Arcad shifted in his seat, smiling at the irony: how pants caught in a strand of barbed wire had ultimately led to this equally tangled set of circumstances.

"That started us off all right. I got us in through a weak point in the barrier, near a boosting station Daddy had told me about once. Then we found a place in town and lived together for almost two years. He didn't go out much, and I couldn't blame him, since it was death for illegal residents in those days. But finally I got bored. I figured if we were going to get caught, why not go out big? Al had always been interested in magic, and he knew quite a few tricks from his sharking days before they broke up Chicago. But he didn't really think in terms of an audience. In fact, his favorite— well, it's not even really a trick, it's a gag—was the rubber-pencil bit. You know, grab a pencil between your thumb and forefinger, wiggle it, and it looks like it's made of rubber. God, the Great Houdini presents his rubber pencil!"

Arcad smirked. "So it was you who got the street act together. Somehow, I can't imagine your husband admitting that."

"Well, it happens to be true. Al's a natural show-off, but it didn't matter to him whether his audience was one, or five, or five million."

"But it does now."

She was apparently unwilling to consider the matter at this moment. Instead, looking over the side as they made their turn over the gate, she grabbed his arm.

"Quick! Set the cut-in at fifty meters—do you know how to do it?"

"Yeah, sure." He twisted the appropriate knob until a green display above the ignition stud indicated fifty meters.

"What are we at now?"

"Fourteen hundred. Why?"

"Here's why!" Lunging, she hit the kill switch. Shuddering slightly, the craft lost inertia. Arcad decided against panic.

"We're dropping."

"Shh! Listen."

There was a quiet rush of air punctuated by the growl of a fog signal as they fell past the top of the twisted south tower and into the fog once more. Arcad started for the ignition, but there *was* something, a sound like the pealing of lead bells far in the distance. This increased until they were surrounded with loud, rhythmic booms, octaves of plucked strings in all tones. One hundred fifty meters, one hundred, seventy-five, fifty—

The inductors did not start up again. Arcad was forced to act quickly, to put them instantly back to two hundred without subjecting their craft to the effects of such acceleration.

Kam was unsure of what had happened, and she shook her head. "How—" she began.

"Fuel surge. What the hell were you doing?"

"Oh, didn't you hear it?" Her eyes glistened, slightly yellow, as she forgot her confusion.

"Hear what?"

"The cables! Since the roadway collapsed, the cables swing free in the wind. They say that on a stormy night it's impossible to sleep around here! If only it were a clear day—"

"How about some warning next time?"

"Yes, *mon général,*" she teased.

Arcad kept his temper—no use becoming another Sterling— but he was amazed by her peaceful, happy expression now that she'd had her way. For all her pragmatic facility, Kam was basically as close to the edge as her husband was.

Or as close as Arcad himself. He sat back and let the beam bring them in for a perfect, hands-off landing. The fog had started burning off, brightening all of San Metro. When he cracked the bubble, Kam handed a bill to the lot attendant, who directed them to an empty slot. Once they parked, she stood up on her seat to check out various boats in the marina slips.

"Good, he's not here yet."

"You think he'll beat us with a boat?"

"It's a hydrofoil, dear, and he might have left a little early. Here." She folded down the seat and pulled at a disk lodged in the storage compartment. "Give me a hand, will you? This is heavy."

"A scooter plat?" Arcad got it onto the ground.

"Well, certainly—you don't expect us to walk, do you? It's almost all the way to Market Street. I've got the bar. You fix the seat and the power packs."

Arcad went to work. The double seat latched on easily, but he had some trouble with the power pack, apparently pirated from a larger model. Eventually, everything was in place; Kam twisted the bar and the disk rose a few centimeters off the ground.

"Dammit, I knew these packs needed charging. Ah, no matter, it should get us there. Hop on."

He settled in hesitantly. With no safety rest or convenient handholds, he was forced to hug her waist to keep himself on the machine. As she'd said, the drained packs gave them a rough ride; once, they hit a protruding slab of asphalt that sent them spinning away like a top-heavy hockey puck. Fortunately, other traffic was light, and when they finally turned onto Van Ness Avenue, where the surface was in better repair, their progress was smoother. Kam weaved through openings provided by more-sluggish vehicles, while Arcad enjoyed the proximity provided by his grip on her.

The avenue was devoted to conspicuous consumption, with appliance stores, hopper and scooter showrooms, restaurants and movie houses, all seemingly well stocked and attractive. Certainly the eastern regions, energy-poor and ravaged by winter each year, had little that was like this. People on the streets were, for the most part, fashionably dressed, walking briskly, intent on the business of the day, presumably unaware that on the other part of the continent misery was thinly spread, not evident specifically, but generally depressing. No wonder these people wanted to control their own affairs. No wonder they'd closed themselves off, refusing to depopulate per order. No wonder Washington was hesitant about a show of force. This society was perhaps the apotheosis of technical efficiency. At the very least it showed a vast improvement over the discredited ways of the past. There was waste here, yes, but it was *calculated,* displayed prominently as a means of economic encouragement. As ever, the cycles were maintained, but in a positive direction: Eat more and you'll make more.

Arcad wondered why more effort was expended in resisting progress than in implementing it. From what he could tell, he was part of the former camp, pledged to bring the West back to the fold, not by changing the East but by reducing the West to the old ways. Suddenly he was annoyed at himself. Always, these implications led to an escalating pyramid of terrible, permanent alteration. With Arcad the unblinking eye atop it all.

They passed the Civic Center. The major quake of the 1990s had demolished the classic beauty of City Hall, leaving only the copper-clad dome, as the first quake had done to its predecessor. This had been shored up, preserved as a monument. The new Metro Center was underground, civil architects having finally learned the lesson of 8.2 Richter.

"Hold on!" Kam yelled, cutting right suddenly onto Grove Street and narrowly avoiding a lorry that had been bearing down in the opposite direction. At the corner of Gough she halted near the door to a three-story brick warehouse, whose antiquated appearance intrigued Arcad.

"This is yours, huh?"

"Al's pride and joy. One of the few brick buildings left in the Metro. Actually, only the frame survived the last shake— it's all eight-by-eight timbers in there. The guy who owned it before us had the brick walls put up again. They'll probably come down the next time too. Come on."

They set the plat next to some other scooters parked by street meters. Kam got a gray plastic rain shroud—"Camouflage," she explained—and covered their machine. Then she went to the building to unlock a single, somewhat grimy door. When Arcad stepped in she locked it behind them. He looked at sunlight angling through dusted air. The first floor was all empty plywood bins.

"Al doesn't like putting anything on street level. There's some crime in the area—more vandalism than anything else, really. We've been broken into a couple of times, but Al's made it difficult to get anything out of here. We can use this floor for office space one of these days, I suppose."

On the way up to the second floor, Arcad noticed that all the joists and floorboards were protected with metal flashing.

"Rats?"

"I beg your pardon! Oh, you mean the metal—that's one of Al's security measures. He goes slightly overboard. Imagines every potential thief to be Houdini himself. Look at the locks on this door."

There were seven of them. Police lock, dead-bolt, padlock and hasp, even one of the new light-magnet combinations.

"You think your husband might have a little trouble getting in without a key?"

She laughed. "Oh, he's called me down a couple of times when he forgot his. Let's see, he numbered them, yeah, five, six—umph—seven. Enter, please."

The second floor was ventilated and, after Kam had switched on the breakers, well lighted. On the far side were heavy machine tools for working both metal and wood. There was even a Johnson miller, quite an antique and apparently in perfect condition. Next to an elevator shaft which was protected by a red metal fire door were stacks of lumber and plywood; on the other side of that, a couple of bins of sheet-metal stock and various grades of aluminum and brass tubing. There were shelves of screws and hardware, an arc-welding generator, tanks for an oxy-acetylene setup, as well as a head for a laser torch.

"Very nice."

"We've had as many as ten people working for us here, when we were producing a big show. . . ." Her voice trailed off. "Now it's him—and sometimes Rusty—working on that." Kam pointed to the center of the shop, where a huge tarp covered what was presently being fabricated.

"That's what he'll be showing them today, I'm sure. Well! Better get to work. Let's see. Yeah, up on the mezzanine there ought to be a big pile of black plush draperies. See if you can hook them to the U-shaped track that comes off the railing there. The hooks are already in. Hopefully it won't be too moth-eaten. It weighs a ton, though, so yell if you need any help."

"What's it for?"

"Stage backdrop. He's doing a presentation and I guess he'll want a little black-on-black work, I'm not sure. All I know is that he wants the water-torture tank filled."

"Okay." Arcad mounted the stairs, found the drapes, and started hooking them onto the track, throwing the parts that were securely fastened over the side. Kam inspected it quickly before wheeling a large glass tank into place in front of the drop with a hand truck. She centered the apparatus, then waited for Arcad to finish with the curtains.

"Good. Now, see the winch and the cord coming down to where you are? It should be wrapped around a couple of nails in the railing. It's a remote switch for the winch."

"You want it down there?"

"Please."

Arcad unwound it, tossing her the bundle with the hand switch on its end. She untangled the knot and tested the mechanism. The overhead motor whirred, and a block and tackle lowered all the way to the floor. Kam then took four open padlocks out of hasps fixed to the metal frame of the cabinet, and flipped up the hasps, which enabled her to lift out a wooden top. This looked like a set of leg stocks with a metal ring between the holes. Kam hooked it to the tackle, checking to see if it was secure. Satisfied finally, she raised the assembly to a level slightly above her head, out of the way.

"Great. Do you see a hose up there—oh, never mind, here it is." She brought it over, stuck it into the tank, and turned on the water. Arcad leaned out to watch the cabinet fill.

"What's this supposed to be?"

Because she was half into a bin, rummaging for something, Kam's voice was muffled, but still understandable.

"It's one of the other Houdini's original bits."

"How's it go?"

"Oh, Al gets clamped by the ankles. We hoist him up, he holds his breath, then into the tank he goes—upside down. I lock the locks, pull a screen, if I can ever—oomph—find the damn thing, in front. And then he escapes in about four minutes."

"He can hold his breath that long?"

She emerged with some white silk bunched in her hands. "Of course not, dummy. He's out in about twenty seconds— half a minute at the most. The rest of the time he sits behind the screen, waiting for the proper hysteria. Usually five or six people faint before the hooded assistant rushes over to break the cabinet—which turns out to be empty. The assistant rips off his hood in amazement, and bingo—it's Houdini."

He stared dreamily as she came up the stairs two at a time toward him, her breasts moving against the rest of her body with ever so slight a delay. He realized he was falling in love with her. It didn't mean anything—in the sense of communication producing change—but he allowed himself to think it all the same. After a while he noticed that she was holding a spool of wire out at him.

"Sorry. What's this?"

"This we're stringing from that metal eye in the wall *there*"—she indicated the place behind him—"down to another near the stage."

"And am I permitted to know the reason?"

She sighed heavily. "Arcad, for someone who's supposed to be a magician, you don't know much."

"My expertise . . . is in other areas."

"I can see you're going to be a big help to me in this."

"I learn fast, though."

"Swell. Here's wire—fasten to eye. Here"—she handed him the silk— "is wire form, covered with a gown that just happens to glow in the dark. This is ghastly mask; long gray hair, see."

Arcad's body tightened with terror. The mask, with its hair, looked too much like his mother. No, he tried telling himself, it isn't she, but his control was slipping away. . . .

Kam saved him. "You all right?"

He closed his eyes, collected himself. "Yeah." He bit his lip. "Yeah. Should have had some breakfast, I guess." He took the form and mask, but deliberately avoided looking at its face again.

"Okay, just hook up the little runner here to the wire. When I give the signal—after things have started—send her down. But hold on to this string. You can control the speed, and when it's almost down, yank hard. The form'll collapse and I can stick it in my shirt or something. The object is this: He's going to be making a serious proposal for this illusion. We're going to turn it into a joke. When you send it down, say something like, 'Sonny! You can't drink that, I haven't boiled it yet.' Then I'll break the cabinet, flood his pals, and make him look like a jerk caught with his locks half open. Got it?"

"I think so."

"Good."

Staring at the flimsy apparatus, Arcad knew the situation had gotten completely out of hand. He was going to be Hamlet in the rafters, ready to unleash a muslin ghost. A very old Hamlet, stuck on the same question, always the same one. Kam started down the stairs.

"Hey," he called after her, "where am I supposed to be during all this?"

"Right where you are, honey, crouching behind the railing like a great big rat."

Kam fastened the wire to the stage, stretching it taut, then running to the breaker panels to bring the lights down enough so the wire couldn't be seen. Arcad opened up the form—which worked something like an umbrella—attached the head (shivering slightly as he did it), and finally clipped the runner to the wire, checking to see that it ran smoothly. It did. He took the specter down, and found a low crate to sit on. His head was just below the top of the railing, but he was able to see through a large knothole.

"Stay right where you are! I think I hear him coming up!" She stepped out of his field of vision to turn off the water.

"Kam!" Sterling's voice came from behind the locked elevator door.

"I'm getting dressed, Al. Have you out in a second." Arcad saw that she had zipped herself into a jet-black coverall. She held a pair of black gloves in one hand as he unlocked the fire door.

"Jesus Christ, you want me to suffocate in there!" Sterling was dressed in a business suit and held a grocery bag. He looked nervous, rocking from foot to foot when he wasn't moving around.

"Here," he said, handing her the bag, "I got some stuff for the guests."

"Mm. Baklava. They'd better get here quick."

"Hey, don't eat that stuff!" Sterling inspected the stage area. "Any problems with the tank?"

"No. You'd better check that inner latch, though. Last time out you said it needed some grease or something, remember?"

"Aaa, it should be okay."

"Al—"

"Come on, let's get the tarp off the new gimmick."

She went over to the side opposite Sterling, then both started pulling and folding, until at last the unfinished framework was exposed. It was a full-scale version of the model Arcad had pocketed yesterday, the same tubular construction in the boom—which was seven or eight meters long. Six carriage bolts provided a mounting for the counterweight. At the other end, only the first fairing and attached cage had been completed so far.

"So this is what you're trying to sell them."

"Exactly."

"And what if they say no?" In spite of her skeptical tone, Arcad could see from the pleasure in her eyes that the new illusion excited her. Because it was new, and because it was his.

"Think positive thoughts. We'll have to go through with it anyway. We're signed. And I've sunk too much money into this thing to back out now. I got both magnets wound last week—guess what that cost."

"You tell me."

"Twenty thousand apiece!"

"Twenty thousand—"

"Out of the advance, relax. Hey, you haven't seen that little model? I thought I left it in my office somewhere."

Kam looked straight up at Arcad. "Uh-uh," she said.

"No? Shit. Well, they ought to get the idea."

"I'm sure they will." She dragged a folded nylon tarp over to a pile of similar material in the corner. When she came back, she was brushing the dust from her arms. Sterling looked at the silk screen which had been placed next to the tank.

"You can take that back."

Kam put her hands on her hips. "You're going to do it in full view?"

"That's right."

"Then you want me to hit the latch for you—"

For the first time he seemed to notice her costume. "No, no black art today. You're spectating with the rest."

"While you show everyone how your best trick is done? Al,

what is it with you? I mean, I'm trying to understand, trying real hard, you know. But I'm not coming up with anything."

"Try shutting up for two minutes."

"I'm listening."

He kissed her cheek. "Look, baby, I need you with me on this. I'm sorry I haven't been straight with you, but you're going to have to trust me. Please. This is bigger than anything we've ever done. Bigger than our relationship—I'm sorry, but it is. But you gotta remember that I still love you."

"It's getting hard."

Sterling waved his hands impatiently. "There's no time for the hearts and flowers, Kam! Look, if you're that upset, we can work in some floating rings just before I go into the tank. I'll spiel about ancient China, home of lost secrets, or something like that."

"Throw the dog a bone," she replied sarcastically, but she also relaxed slightly.

"Jesus H. Christ, girl—"

"Simmer down." Kam patted the top of his head. "Rings it is. Don't worry, I won't spoil your show. But you and I are going to do some serious talking when we get home, *comprende?*"

"Thanks, babe, I knew you'd come through!" He whirled around. "Let's see, we got to get some chairs set up—and is that coffeemaker still around here someplace?"

Arcad watched the two of them work. They were good together, very good, each anticipating the other's movements, reaching across at the right time, never getting in the way. Was anything worth more than such rapport? It was, on a physical level, something like the way he and Nukhulls had operated in planning and execution. He remembered the way they'd separated an oil-shale lobbyist from two key, overly greedy committeemen back in D.C. The look on that man's face as his precious nuclear-percolation bill was defeated—with the two swing votes coming from what he thought were his own men—had given Arcad much satisfaction. Accomplishment, in whatever context: that was what gave meaning to life, made it more than an interminable play in a theater of one. The smell of coffee made his stomach growl suddenly. He should have eaten. Kam practiced a few moves with her five chrome rings, switching around the two permanently linked rings with the key and the other two loose ones.

A buzzer went off, which kicked Sterling into action.

"That's them. I'm going to bring 'em up in the elevator. Cut the lights a little more, and get some spots on the boom, and on the tank there. I don't want 'em thinking they're wasting their morning in a cheap toy factory." As he ran off to the elevator shaft, Arcad stood up painfully to stretch.

"You still want me to send the dummy down," he said dryly.

Kam looked up. "Don't be a smart-ass."

"Just wondering. After all these heated protestations."

"Shh! They're coming up." Quickly she adjusted the lighting per Sterling's instructions. Once again Arcad sat down on the crate, watching Kam gather the energy necessary to deliver on her social obligations. In the limited field visible through the knothole, Arcad was able to recognize Peter Deliewe by his Vandyke. Besides the governor and Sterling, there were three others for Kam to greet.

"Ah, Peter. Dragged kicking and screaming from your desk."

"No," Deliewe said, bussing her cheek, "I've actually been looking forward to this all morning. Kam, here's the guy you could hear yelling. Tom Stassen, from Fresno. Tom, meet Al and Kam Sterling."

"Tom—" Sterling shook his hand.

"Pleased to meet you." Stassen, a bald man, examined his surroundings with some distaste.

"And, Kam, you remember Jerry Parsons and Cornell Brown."

"From the Planning Commission. We're honored. Will you gentlemen have a seat? There's coffee, pastry—that is, if you're not afraid of spoiling lunch."

"If you don't mind," said Stassen, "I'd like to get under way. I've got a committee report to deliver in forty-five minutes."

Deliewe grinned. "Tom's our most dependable critic. I think he's been playing devil's advocate for so long they've offered him the head job. But I'll have a cup. How about you, Cornell? Jerry?"

"Three cups?" Sterling poured and served the beverage himself, with Kam following up with the pastry. Even Stassen did not pass up the baklava. Very quietly, Kam withdrew to the side; Sterling waited for his guests to settle themselves.

At the proper moment he clapped his hands. "All right! As they used to say in Agatha Christie's books, I suppose you are all wondering why I've called you here today. I won't be so coy as her Inspector Poirot, however. I know the commission's coming up on a decision concerning something I'm personally involved in—the big show that's being broadcast from back East on July Fourth. Since you haven't yet approved a west coast hook-up, I thought it would be courteous—at the very least—to explain what I'll be doing, and to show you something else. Something I think as politicians you'll be very interested in."

"Ah, excuse me, Mr. Sterling." Stassen leaned far back in his chair. "Before we get too far along, I've heard some things concerning your contractual arrangement with the July Fourth Committee in Washington. Is it true that your overall fee, exclusive of expenses, increases by a full third if our region accepts the network feed?"

"Jesus Christ, Tom—"

Sterling held up a hand magnanimously. "No, Peter, it's a fair question. That's quite correct, Mr. Stassen, and the reason for that is the simple increase in advertising revenue. I'm being paid a percentage. I don't feel free to give out dollar amounts—only to say that I have performed for less. And for much more. After all, my segment will be only fifteen minutes or so. If you knew me better, you'd understand—and I think my friends here will agree—that money doesn't mean very much to me,

97

not at this stage of my career. There are other things in life. . . . Ah, but as you've said, Mr. Stassen, this really isn't the time to discuss my material philosophy. Let's just say that my compensation covers expenses."

Sterling walked over to his boom.

"This is part of the apparatus which I will employ for the effect. I'd hoped to show you a model of the whole rig, but I couldn't find it. Which shows you not even magicians can conjure up everything they want. Anyway, this"—he patted the tubing—"is my Passage Through Molten Silver. Not very impressive at the moment. But I've always maintained that props should not get in the way of the performer.

"The effect will be performed in earth orbit, which may seem overly dramatic, not to mention expensive, but unfortunately it's the only place this illusion can be physically performed. There will be, let's see, twenty-four, no, twenty-six separate camera pods more or less spherically arranged to provide full coverage. Also, a shuttle for staging both my crew and the video people, and another for the committee of experts who will verify the authenticity of my equipment. Then there'll be one or two converted space labs reserved for those who were conspicuously generous in the last political campaign."

All four men laughed. Houdini had captured yet another audience.

"I'll explain the setup so you'll understand what I'm going to try." Sterling grabbed one of the carriage bolts. "Down at this end we'll have a big concrete mass around which this thing will revolve once it's up there. Incidentally, total payload on this baby will be something like one hundred and eighty metric tons—and you should have seen the face on the guy from government accounting when he heard that! It's costing forty-five C.U. dollars a kilo to orbit the thing. Anyway, you've got the boom, and then the other end, where all the good stuff will be happening. This cage is for me. Inside we'll have a pulley-and-line arrangement leading to another cage at the very end. Between that . . . well, Jerry, you're the financial expert: Sterling silver's still holding at $8.20, am I right?"

"Eight point one nine eight per decagram," said Parsons.

"Well boys, I've liquidated most of my fortune. At home, sitting on a pallet just as shiny as you please, are exactly 64,470 one-kilogram ingots, worth, at that $8.20 figure, $52,-865,400.00. Won't say where I got it, other than telling you I pulled an exchange—not exactly to my advantage—of some securities with a middle eastern friend I impressed at a solo performance a few years back. Materialized a lady he'd been interested in from a cage suspended over what he called his throne. I'm taking that silver into space with me.

"It's going to be magnetically suspended between the two cages and then heated by a battery of lasers to a temperature of 960.8 Celsius, at which point it will liquify and assume a spherical shape with an exact diameter of 2.27 meters. That line I told you about will be running through it. And then we'll have the familiar scenario. I'm going to be hot-tied and clipped to that line, which will then pull me s l o w l y toward the silver. Think of it!" Houdini put his hands behind his back, twisting his shoulders as if he really were trying to wiggle out of knotted cord. "There I am! One leg free! The other! I'm getting closer, I'm almost in, right arm"—he held it up high, eyes wide—"but I just can't get that last wrist. Instead, I'm pulled in."

Quickly Sterling hopped over the boom framework so that he was out of the view of the others, though Arcad could still see him.

"Think of it! This thing goes around. And around. One minute. Two minutes. Now everyone is just starting to believe I'm fried. People scream, horror, panic! Committee members and my crew come out of their ships to help, though they've got no idea what they can possibly do to save me. Then all of a sudden—" He stepped around the end of the cage, smiling radiantly. "All of a sudden I come out. Baptized by molten metal. *Changed.*"

The way Alphonse Sterling said the word *changed* chilled

Arcad to the deepest part of him. He had a very bad feeling about what was going on here. . . .

Deliewe broke the silence. "Changed? Changed how?"

"I'll answer that with a question of my own. Peter, what if you had the ability to make a statement—anything at all— and be absolutely certain you'd be believed, no matter what the truth? And more than that, what if those who believed you were willing to act on that faith?"

"I imagine my love life might improve."

"I call it a nightmare," Stassen mumbled.

Sterling jumped to the response. "Granted, Mr. Stassen— if that power lies in the wrong hands. If you will bear with me, gentlemen, I'm going to demonstrate that dream can be reality, with the help of that piece of equipment you see on the little stage in front of you. Lights, please!"

The warehouse was darkened almost completely, with only the tank's dim glow providing a point of reference. Against it, Arcad saw a black figure rush past, Kam, wearing a black hood. Against the black curtain, as long as she stayed away from the tank, it would be almost impossible to see her from the floor. From his own position, however, her form was fairly distinct against the lighter stage. With precise, snapping movements she started working the rings; her husband provided the narration:

"Beginning on a theme of China. Curious, the role that ancient nation played in the arena of politics and in that of its close ally, entertainment."

Kam held two outside rings with the three others suspended between. Arcad was impressed by her grip—a kind of three-fingered pinch—which kept her gloves from showing up against the chrome. By bending her wrists, she made the whole arrangement blossom into a globe of interconnected arcs, which she quickly threaded onto a short string. Deliewe and the others suddenly saw it spin, suspended in mid-air.

"The minds that invented this no longer exist. Victims of the armed forces of our former nation. A pity. Snuffed out."

Kam covered the rings suddenly with a black cloth and ran offstage, removing her jumpsuit and donning a gray cowl. She put down the hood, walked back onstage, and smiled. Houdini led the applause.

"Thank you, my dear. What you saw, gentlemen, seemed unreal, impossible. But, ultimately, explainable, which is perhaps the reason why the Chinese could not prevail. They stopped. Became too satisfied with the world as it was. They did not progress; they learned how to convey the illusion of reality from the apparent, but they did not care to coalesce that illusion. Perhaps they considered such a refusal to be the basis of a noble philosophy. But in a world that was all too harsh, their attitude was sadly unrealistic. I do not intend repeating that mistake. My own research has continued, and by a combination of technique and a certain innate ability, I am able to produce *at will* what you are about to witness. Gentlemen, you shall have reality imposed upon you. Please, check that first impression. And restrain yourself from doing anything you might think is immediately necessary. Kam, if you would be so kind as to help me with my jacket."

Arcad judged it safe to stand, and when he did he saw Sterling's shirt eerily reflecting the tank light. He attached the form runner to the wire, hoping as he did so that Kam could keep her husband from tripping over it. She did, guiding him to the side of the water-torture tank. By means of the switch, she lowered the ankle stocks to the floor. Houdini lay down, and removed his shoes and socks before allowing her to clamp him in. Then he took the switch himself and raised the tackle slowly, with Kam steadying him with the flats of both hands. When he was upside down directly above the tank, with his hair touching water, he handed the control to Kam and spoke again.

"I'd like you to think about death for a moment. This tank is a copy of the one invented by the great Harry Houdini, my distinguished predecessor and namesake. In his time he was the greatest escape artist that had yet lived. But he was unable to solve that final problem. What man does not think himself immune to the ghastly call from the beyond? But even Harry was unable to conquer that last barrier. Escape was impossible for him, for anyone—until I discovered a way to help." He looked at Kam, who acknowledged him with a serious, amazed nod.

"Okay! Let's not forget about life. To remind you what I'm doing, I'd like you to see if you can hold your breath as long as the Great Houdini can. Kam will call out thirty-second intervals. Ready—"

With a splash, Houdini went chest-deep into the tank and hung there, eyes open and cheeks puffed. Arcad was holding his breath, though he felt weak and sickened by the energy present in the room.

"Thirty seconds!"

If there had been any way out at all, Arcad would have left. His head pounded, the air in his lungs as trapped as he was.

"One minute."

Down below, breath was being released in rushes that sounded almost like tires exploding. Arcad too was forced to let go; leaning against the railing, he puffed and tried fighting the spots that swam in front of his eyes.

"One minute thirty!"

Jesus, God, no one could hold it like this! At two minutes thirty, Houdini twisted slightly, a signal for Kam to raise him. Water streamed from the illusionist's body as he emerged.

"And now," he gasped, "the test! One! Two! Three! In!"

He slammed into the water, Kam locking the padlocks two at a time. Cheeks puffed, he folded his arms serenely, making no effort to escape.

The lights in the tank went off.

And fire burned above it. Kam jumped back to stare at the light of a human head surrounded by a shimmering aura. Arcad blinked, discarding possibilities as he felt the surge of energy that was not his own. No other wires. No projectors, no doubles. Only the tank, the head, and the astounded glow in the eyes of the Regional Planning Commission.

Then from the head came a voice that had a strong eastern accent. "Hello. I can't see all of you clearly—conditions are not the best, as I'm just back from what some would call a long vacation. Took a little longer to collect myself than I thought."

Not a single bubble had yet risen to the top of the tank. Arcad gave his wire form one look, then threw it to the floor. If only he didn't feel so weak!

"Oh, I exist all right. I'm as real in my own way as you are in yours. Which is not as real as you think. You feel that I'm here, Mr. Stassen?"

"What kind of trick is this—"

The head shifted slightly. "Your skepticism is strong—but fortunately not strong enough to do harm to our mutual friend in the tank. Look at him. He's quite literally suspended, and will remain so as long as you believe.

"But, to the question: I am the other Houdini, Harry Houdini. And you might say I'm a sales representative at the moment. So, please relax."

A great calm washed over the room, affecting those seated on the floor. Stassen's arms dropped to his side.

"He wanted me to ask that you examine your feelings right now. They are altered, are they not? You know you want to be worried, but you *can't*. And you know you can't but don't care, isn't that correct? Well, know too—and you do believe me—that we can produce any emotion we choose, and you will be caught absolutely in its grip. Think of high rage, hysterical sorrow, fear, ecstasy. You feel a touch of each of them, am I right?" The aura flared green on its fringes.

And Sterling still hadn't moved. Hamlet still, Arcad gripped the rail.

"The point, gentlemen—and my lady—is that we can produce any type of emotion in a group of any size. We can charge the spirit, lay essential belief to waste, produce the fervent need to act, religiously, artistically, and, what must interest you most, politically. Consider this: What if you wished to convince your constituency of the importance of a certain course of action? With a speech and a great amount of organization, you might get the support of a few, the interest of a few more. Hardly gratifying, without considering the troublesome problem of dealing with opposition, which is certain to arise no matter what the question.

"But we now have the capacity to rid you of this political inefficiency. We can produce any great figure of the past to exhort the masses. *And they will believe!*"

"Freedom of choice . . ." whispered Stassen hoarsely.

"Is a dangerous freedom for those who lack the necessary information. Even you, Mr. Stassen, for all your blowing about individual rights, set yourself above the rest in your official capacity. Will you ally yourself with the political charlatans of the past as an amateur playing with forces you don't comprehend? I understand that your Adolf Hitler once practiced his devilish oratory before a mirror; he might well have broken every mirror he owned to insure his ultimate success! The inner reflection matters, gentlemen!

"You are leaders, all of you, like it or not. And it remains to be seen whether your generation is capable of exercising perfect authority wisely. Or are you afraid? Is it that you secretly count on the disruptions produced by entrenched minorities? The sluggish confusion of bureaucrats? Your own finely carved consciences? Do you actually hope for these impedances in order to avoid having to accept responsibility for your actions? Those days are over. Gentlemen, we offer you Excalibur. Will you throw it aside in favor of your own rusted pocketknives?"

The head had grown in size and power. There was no mistaking it now; somehow, Sterling was projecting the entity while suspending his own life processes. Nukhulls' suspicions were correct, and it was time now for Arcad to do what he had been sent to do. This time there would be no remorse. He concentrated on his breathing, preparing to bore in on Sterling's puppet show with his own tremendous energy. When he was ready, he projected it with all his strength.

There was resistance. Resistance to the point of his own limits. The will to strip Alphonse Sterling of this new power had somehow been diverted—at physical cost, however: the illusionist was thrashing inside the tank. And the head of Harry Houdini whirled back, searing Arcad with his incomparable gaze.

"You interfere!" the voice screamed.

The wave of force thrown up at him was overwhelming; Arcad was physically hurled against the mezzanine wall. Shocked, he tried gathering his power again, sucking energy from every part of his body. Again he projected, screaming as he did it. The tank rocked on its legs.

"Believe, damn you!"

"Aahh!" Arcad reached out for an anchor, something to tie him to the present, to keep him from being utterly destroyed. He did believe . . . until he saw what he held in his hands. There was the mask, the gray hair. It was Mother, and they were trying to kill her again. "Save yourself!" he screamed, and she rose out of him, taking form with one sad, loving glance at her fallen son. Floating to the floor, Mother confronted the other specter.

"This must stop!" She pointed at the head of Houdini. "The fault is yours. Go back."

"No!" screamed the voice, but already the head was shrinking, moving back from her. Sterling hung limp—

"Yesssss!" The tank exploded, water rushing over the frozen audience. The lights came on all at once, and Kam was shrieking, "Al, Al!"

Still suspended by the ankles, Sterling's body twisted slowly as she ran to him. Lowering him quickly, she put her ear to his chest, then pounded it a few times until he started thrashing again. She gripped his wrists to calm him.

"It's all right, darling, I'm here, it's all right. . . ."

Coughing up water, Sterling sat up, weak but triumphant. "Well?" he asked.

Deliewe finally seemed to remember where he was. Stassen stared at the floor, which was now completely dry.

"What message can you give us?" he asked.

"Whatever the board decides, sir. And whatever spokesman you want, we can get. I can get Richard Nixon, if that's what you want."

Above them, Arcad picked himself up from the mezzanine floor. Mother had returned, and he wanted to hear more. He saw Kam looking up at him with hatred in her eyes. If she now knew about her husband, she knew all about Arcad too. That was too painful. He had thought himself in love with her.

There was still enough left in Arcad for him to get out without being seen. Little power was needed anyway, because of the way all of them were chattering around Sterling. Ever able to capitalize, Sterling was in control again as plans were formulated.

Arcad wondered, as he stalked the streets, numb, if he should have expected anything else.

8.

Arcad lay on his back under some trees in Yerba Buena Park, just south of Mission Street. Through the eucalyptus branches he could see small, rapidly moving clouds appear and disappear. The shapes were interesting, built up according to a hierarchy of conditions which had been, for convenience' sake, described as physical laws, even though they weren't really laws at all. Laws could be instituted, altered, stricken. Interpreted, as these conditions could never be. For that reason, God himself had no laws; only divine acquiescence, or laziness.

He felt a little better, having eaten a sandwich purchased from a vendor's stand at the Sixth Street gateway to the park. At the time, he had wanted to get away from the tall buildings of the financial district. The thought of all the people inside them, working on figures, or objects which they controlled with the aid of tools, pencils, their own hands, filled him with despair. Every one of those people concentrated on a universe that wasn't much more than one meter square. They devoted all their energy toward this field, blocking out all other thoughts, and why not? The imagination was chained to the physical body. Why speculate on larger considerations when one was occupied already? How lucky they were! Arcad's problem was that he had to *force* himself to concentrate on particulars. His physical body had been chained to a narrowed imagination.

It was much easier to accept limits imposed than to impose those limits oneself. Especially when those limits extended to others.

"Hi," came a tiny voice.

He squinted up. A little girl with soft brown hair, wearing a green sweatshirt, stood over him, holding a yellow ball.

"Hi," he answered.

"Are you sick, sir?"

"What's that?" Seeing that she was, in a way, concerned, he managed a smile. "Oh. I'm a little tired. But the grass is nice to sit on, isn't it?"

She shook her head. "It's all wet." Fingering a loose tooth, she examined him a moment longer. "My mommy said I wasn't supposed to talk to you."

"She's probably right."

"Uh-uh."

Arcad sat up. "Hon, where is your mommy?"

"At home."

"Then you should listen to her. You might meet someone who doesn't like little girls." Or likes them too much, he thought.

"No, I won't."

"Yeah? And how do you know?"

"Easy." She laughed, hitting his knee. "I can tell if you're nice. Want to play?"

"I don't think so—not right now."

"Why not?"

"Because I have to call somebody. You be careful, though." Arcad watched her run over to a drinking fountain. The girl had good instincts, which she ought to be allowed to trust. Even though it was so easy to make a mistake.

He walked over to the nearest phone booth and rang up Nukhulls. The blue Confederal logo came onscreen.

"Party and caller, please."

"Nukhulls. From Ryan Arcad."

There was about a minute's delay. Finally Nukhulls appeared, looking pale. His eyes were quite red.

"Arcad! George was starting to wonder about you."

"How is he?"

"Great. That damned cat eats more than I do. So what's up?"

Arcad swallowed. "I found out what you wanted to know."

"Go on."

"It's going to be in orbit, as you said. I've got a model of the apparatus, and a running description. I'll make the formal report when I get in." He thought he heard George purring over the line, and he wished desperately that both he and his cat were home. Maybe Nukhulls would let him go. . . .

"That's it?"

"No. No, you were right about the other thing too. Sterling is psychokinetic."

"How? Exactly how?"

"I don't know—it's different from mine. Very powerful. Images and some kind of compulsion; I suppose I could duplicate the effect, but not at the strength I saw. Now, whether he's also using some equipment, I don't know."

Nukhulls didn't exactly smile, but there definitely was happiness in those narrowed eyes.

"All right," he said. "What's your opinion?"

"That he's a dangerous man."

"And did you do anything about it?"

"I tried to burn it out of him this morning, but I lost control. His resistance was incredible. Mother . . ." He fought off the dizziness that that memory produced. "Mother came out and broke things up. But Sterling's intact and my cover's blown."

"I see." Nukhulls did not comprehend Arcad's failure, but lack of success could always be attributed to a lack of proper planning. "What do you suggest, then?"

"How the hell should I know! If he can do what I saw him

109

do today—to large numbers of people. . . . Get them to drop him."

"That won't solve the problem."

"No, but for right now it will keep him from doing what he's got in mind. I don't care what you do—just get the July Fourth Committee to fire him."

"Arcad, I thought you understood that there's no question of doing that, there never has been. You're going to have to act."

"Don't you understand, he's stronger than me!"

"All I understand is that I need him to perform that illusion. There's a lot more than your weakness at stake here. Jesus, he's just an overblown entertainer! You don't have to do anything drastic—just make sure he remains an entertainer."

"You promised me no one would get hurt. . . ."

"I haven't said a thing about you hurting anyone."

"Well, that's what's going to happen!"

"Look. I understand you've lost a battle. That's what's really bothering you, isn't it? You've never had the experience. Just think of it as character building—"

"Don't give me that bullshit!"

Nukhulls frowned. "All right, take it this way: Your orders are to neutralize him. In whatever way is necessary. Orders, Arcad—have I made myself clear?"

"I can walk out of town right now—"

"And I'll find you no matter where you try to hide. I'll bring you back; by God, you're going to finish this job." Nukhulls held the cat up to the screen. "You want to see George again, don't you?"

Arcad broke the connection suddenly and left the phone booth. Across the path, the little girl bounced her ball in front of another stranger, a stranger who did not look at all friendly. By pushing out a little with his mind, he made her ball bounce away from potential trouble. Opening up some more, Arcad put the image of Mommy into the girl's mind. She twirled lightly and skipped away toward the townhouses at the edge of the park.

He was gratified by his success. His power was his life. If it did not prevail, there was no Ryan Arcad. He felt in his pocket for change, so that he could make the hopper back to Pacifica.

God damn the Nukhullses of the world.

9.

At the moment of sexual climax there is a wish to die. Life's work has been completed, the body is nothing more than a spent, decaying vessel, its demise somewhat hastened by the energy thus expended. It is at this point that the illusion of control becomes a joke, an evaporation.

But not for Ryan Arcad. And now it was the same for Sterling. The two of them lived alone in a world which had no right to exist. All his life Arcad had fought to escape from that world, without success. How, then, could he hope to force Sterling out?

It was almost dark by the time he climbed the hill leading up the Slide. He had seen the rock from several miles away, where it appeared to be pinned to the air in the gray dusk. There was no sign of activity anywhere on the property. Now it began to rain; cold pellets were lashed across his face by an unforgiving wind. Then the wind picked up, really hurting. As an exercise, Arcad kept it off, feeling a sensation something like that of a hand pressing against a wind-filled sail. He dried his face, then tried warming up a little, realizing as he did so that he was dangerously weary. The sandwich in the park had not stood him very long, but there was nothing to be done now. He could hardly present himself and inquire whether he was late for dinner.

Pausing in the shelter of a tilted boulder, Arcad thought about Kam. He remembered the look of hatred on her face and wanted to tell her that this whole thing wasn't his fault. Of course, he'd nearly killed her husband. But what about the plot she'd hatched, her intended humiliation of the illusionist. Her silent indictment was so unfair, and yet, in a way, he understood it. Arcad had gone after the one thing she still had—Alphonse Sterling. If he had succeeded, perhaps she would have been satisfied, but, as it was, failure made him despicable. The noble lines about his eyes had become the cringe folds of a simpering coward; his careful discretion, plain inadequacy. Never mind that, in essence, she had planned to do to her husband almost exactly what had occurred anyway.

She knew very well what the difference was. It was very sad.

The pad lights came on suddenly, and Arcad realized he had no exact plan. He decided to go to the museum; according to Kam, it was the location of Sterling's recent intense meditations. Perhaps there would be a clue contained therein which would help him overcome the greater power of Alphonse Sterling.

Go, he thought, crawling silently along the path to the loading dock. He got the door open without much trouble—though it squeaked loudly—slipped in, and closed it behind him. Kam's hopper was back. Probably she had returned alone while Sterling and Deliewe closeted themselves to make plans.

Except that she couldn't fly.

Which meant that they both were here. Arcad wondered just who he might pray to for help. *After abdicating the godhead himself?* Drawing on his reserves, he melted the lock on the inner door. The bolt dropped away and he entered the museum, which was lit in dim red, as it had been the last time. Cautiously he followed the spiral corridor past the displays. Illusion, change, misguided perception, all of it was here, all of it meant nothing. Something brushed his cheek—

But he did not cry out. It was only the loose arm of a leering, glass-eyed dummy tilted on a stand above his shoulder. He caught his breath, then continued the spiral inward until he reached the door to the Ehrich Weiss Collection. It was open.

"Come in, come in."

Sterling's voice!

Arcad stepped through to confront a figure straight in front of him. The face was that of the floating head from the Gough Street warehouse: Harry Houdini stood there, dapper in a short-sleeved forked coat, winged collar, and spats. He smiled ludicrously. In his hands he held a large paper ring bearing his monicker in archaic script. His expression was one of knowledge and supreme confidence, frozen forever in wax. It was only a replica.

"The central attraction at last!"

"Sterling?"

The illusionist stepped out from behind a wall of brick that lay next to a lathe gazebo, which Arcad remembered from the picture in Sterling's office. He was stripped to the waist, his compact musculature revealed. Arcad gauged his smile: contemptuous, with a touch of pity; above all, as confident as his wax namesake. Arcad hooded his eyes with his hands, as if he were staring at a white-hot metal statue instead of at a man.

"You seem to have recovered," he commented.

"After spitting out a couple of liters, yes. I've been waiting for you."

"What if I hadn't come?"

"I wouldn't have been waiting."

"Glib enough, but you can cut it: I'm not in the fan club."

"No." Sterling seemed to relax slightly. "You're not."

"And I think we both know how things stand."

"That, my friend, remains to be seen. Step in, close the door. Not many people have been inside this little sanctuary."

Arcad sniffed the air. "This is the good stuff, huh?"

"This is Harry's stuff. All of it that still exists, that is. Political disorder is not conducive to the preservation of artifacts,

I'm afraid. But some things got through to me all right. Look around."

"I like your friend there."

Sterling patted Harry's head with pride. "This is from Madame Tussaud's in London. It was on display during his lifetime. The local commissar called it decadent, but he gave it to me anyway. Perhaps he's hoping it'll bore the fatal wormhole into the foundations of state capitalism!" He laughed, a little too loudly.

"Anyway, it shows Harry in his prime. About 1910, 1911. Before his mother's death redirected him to an unhealthy obsession with the activities of the spiritualist movement."

"You two don't look much alike."

Sterling glanced back at the replica. "No, not really. We're about the same size. But his face is more . . . European. But here"—he thumped his chest with his fist"—we're just the same."

"Hollow?"

"You got a big mouth, you know that?"

Arcad sat down as Sterling decided to continue.

"No, we both know how to put people right where we want. Look at him! Even in wax he's scary. His whole career consisted of getting away with murder. He'd do his stuff right in front of people's noses and have them swearing that he was a real wizard."

"Was he?"

"I used to think so. Now . . ." Sterling lit a cigarette and offered one to Arcad, which he declined. "I'm not sure. I do think that anyone who can manipulate in the way he did is probably half there as it is. It's a gift, making strangers share your concerns. It takes knowledge, and some kind of ability to project the will. Take that, for example."

He pointed to a stamped metal five-pointed star set upon a rococo brass stand. "The card star. That wasn't one of Harry's inventions, but he liked to use it in the early days. It's based on a technique called a force, usually done with a deck of cards. Here. I want you to pick a card. As they say, any card."

Sterling fanned a deck in front of Arcad, who selected a three of clubs.

"All right." Sterling pointed his finger toward the prop. "See the cord down here? Just yank it with my foot, and bang—" The three of clubs appeared on the uppermost point.

"Let me guess. The whole deck is the three of clubs."

"Take a look. No, the deck is okay, but it's stacked, insofar as I knew the position of the five cards matching what's sprung behind the star. But the trick is in the force. Think about it. You wanted to choose what you thought was the least obvious pick, in case I was trying to 'make' you pick the right one. The cards were arranged in a kind of order of preference. Some I jacked out just a little; some were pulled in. The best choice from your point of view was also the right choice for me. That's the force. And it'll work eight times out of ten if it's done right. Now what would you call that, Arcad? A lucky guess? Good psychology? Or applied willpower?"

"I'd say a combination of all three."

Sterling blew smoke at him. "But then, you're not a legitimate performer."

"And you are."

"Nothing but. See, I know what to do with people's expectations, just like Harry did. I set 'em up, get 'em looking the right way, then use their preconceptions against them."

"You're a professional liar."

"In a way. Only, people leave my shows happy. They want to be fooled, that's why they come to see me! Look at it this way: Every day the regular guy gets screwed. He's always being told that he doesn't know enough, or that he's made another mistake, misread some important piece of paper. I show him that it's all right to miss things, it's natural, and furthermore it makes life more interesting. I'm appreciated."

"But that's not enough anymore, is it, Sterling?"

The illusionist shrugged. "Folks is still getting screwed. Even if I make them feel good about it for a while. I began wondering if there wasn't something more I could do. I mean, I could keep on doing what I was doing, but then I'd be abdicating my responsibility to use my fame and position toward change. But if I left the stage to work in that direction, I'd be depriving my audience of one of the few pleasures they could count on. So I started thinking about new ways. All of us do it. Harry here went on a fifteen-year crusade against the spiritualists. The funny thing was, he really wanted to believe. He was dying for his mother to contact him from the netherworld. When he didn't get the results he hoped for, he began an attack that pretty much discredited the whole movement. He exposed all the fakes. But he also got a few people who were genuinely talented in that direction, mostly because he was able to duplicate, by mechanical means, any of the so-called contacts from the other side.

"That soured him. If he could do it, there were no spirits involved, and his traveling inquisition put an end to what he thought were crooks mining false hopes. Harry made one mistake, though. He assumed that these fakes were as good as he was—you know, could do all the sleights, ring the bell with their feet, produce the palmed apports. Many of them were as good; but then, some were not."

"Some were genuine."

"Exactly. And those people interested me. I began to see the possibilities. What if a man with the experience and instincts of a performer was capable of producing and controlling psychic phenomena."

"I'd say you'd have one hell of a show."

"I'd say you'd have a person capable of instituting and controlling social change. Think of it! Most people have plans for themselves, expectations, which are usually not met. These people force themselves to settle for less. Their ambition is blunted by diversion—by entertainment, I'll admit that—intermediate pleasures whose per-unit cost is low enough for society to dole them out in insufficient quantity. Now, what if someone came along who could convince these people that their temporary satisfaction was strangling them! And more, that the power to change was within, lacking only direction to become an irresistible force—"

"I've heard the rest of this, Sterling."

"Yes, you have, haven't you." The magician put out his cigarette. "From your tone, I take it you don't approve."

"You're not concerned with my approval."

"No, but I'm trying to be considerate . . . to a potential partner."

Arcad's surprise showed. "You're not serious."

"You're disappointing me, Arcad. I'd hoped you'd be anxious to compare notes, see how I developed my own ability. That moment when you first knew you were different—isn't that something you've always wanted to share?"

There was a dim memory. . . . Arcad, on the floor, watching his black kitten play with a scattered deck of cards. Come here, little kit, here, here—and the little body turned, helpless, eyes gone powder blue, the pointed ears hidden by long silver hair, the mouth stuck on—no, no, no. . . .

Arcad shook his head, trying to clear his brain. Sterling smirked.

"I'm not so selfish; I'll tell you about mine. For eight years I tried. At least two hours a day I'd come here and look at him. All I wanted was a wink. I tried every technique I could read about. Concentration. No concentration. Projection. Obliteration of the self. And one day I felt this *thing* come out of nowhere, grabbing hold of my brain. Then all of a sudden Harry was here, babbling about the other side, what he'd been doing, what I could do. My entire personality was stripped away—"

"I don't believe you!"

"You like to think you're the only person in this world who has to struggle. I know all about you! I did from the first."

"That's a lie."

"Convince yourself, it's all right. You're a cream puff. I knew what was up when I saw you and your friend at the party.

It was interesting. Then, you frightened me a little, because I wasn't strong enough yet. But Harry helped me along. Then I wanted to see how far I could go before you'd try taking me on. Fortunately, you waited. And now I'm in a position to offer you employment."

Arcad could only stare, mouth open.

"Don't answer right away; think of the possibilities first. You've got range, but you lack direction. Together, we'll be able to make the world whatever we want. End all the stupidity, right now!"

"No," Arcad said calmly.

"I know, you've got your scruples. Harry told me you were a tortured soul. Something about a murder."

Arcad's composure disintegrated. "It was an accident!" he cried. "She surprised me and I couldn't help. . . ." He stopped, suddenly confused, as if the memory of his mother's death was not at all real. "We don't have the right. . . ."

Sterling snorted contemptuously. "Don't have the guts is more like it. Or maybe you're a fake yourself. Harry says no, but I'm starting to wonder."

"I don't have anything to prove."

"Ah, but I insist. Here." Sterling pulled a cloth off what looked like a desk but was in reality a pallet stacked with tarnished silver bars. Sterling picked one up, testing its weight. He threw it to Arcad.

"Do something with that."

"No."

"Would you prefer a little struggle of wills? I'm not distracted like I was this afternoon."

I've got to humor him, Arcad realized, give myself time to get set, let him think he's in control. . . . He concentrated on the structure of the silver. There was a feeling of compression, of building heat, which he quickly dissipated. Arcad could almost visualize the alchemical transformation. The bar felt heavier. He threw it back to Sterling, who nearly dropped it.

"Now that's a hell of a note—solid gold! You're going to have to teach me that one. Talent or no talent, money makes it easier to lubricate the opposition."

"I'm not teaching you anything." He watched as Sterling ran his finger over the lacquered frame of a Japanese shoji screen.

Then he winked theatrically at Arcad. "Remember what I said about preconceptions working against reality? You, Arcad, for instance, imagine that I don't mean business. A serious mistake. Behind this screen is a glass cabinet about the size of a cedar chest. Harry's crystal water casket. It's all bound in heavy brass, with locks and straps securing the top. Because it's so small, there's a little bubble built into the top to make room for the performer's head. It's a perfect example of Harry's way. Everyone concentrates on the locks, not realizing that it only takes a half-twist of the bubble to free the glass from the brass binding. Sounds simple, doesn't it? But still dangerous. There's very little air in that bubble, if anything goes wrong."

Laughing, he pulled away the panel. Kam was inside, gasping desperately because of the depleted air supply. She looked wildly toward Arcad, who was too stunned to do anything immediately.

"Sterling! She's got nothing to do with this!"

"Oh, but she has. Look at the way her hair floats, like spun coral it looks! She told me everything. How you agreed to aid her pathetic attempt to make a fool out of me. And you went along, didn't you? You wanted to get by without having to do anything yourself, isn't that it?"

"For the love of God, she's drowning!"

"So she is. A pity."

Unable to wait any longer, Arcad caused all four locks to spring open. Sterling countered quickly, closing them again. Arcad then concentrated on the glass, got a grip on it, making it thinner and thinner, but then the resistance came. Kam went under the water in the tank. Arcad screamed and lunged for a silver bar, intending to smash the glass with it—

But Sterling stuck a hypo into his arm, just below the shoulder muscle. Arcad turned, just as the drug started to affect him. He threw the bar, which thudded uselessly against the glass.

The illusionist's eyebrows arched above his glistening eyes. "Your friend Nukhulls used this drug on occasion, I believe. You're like the rest of them now."

"Kam," he whispered, falling to his knees. He tried fighting the parogen, but it was no good; he'd been surprised and now it was too late. His center of control grew smaller and smaller still, until it was sealed off from him. Wobbling, he watched Sterling unscrew the bubble from the top of the casket.

"Oh, there you are, my dear. Unfortunately, he refused to consider my proposition." The locks popped open again, but this time Sterling pulled them through their hasps so that he could remove the top. Kam shot from her bier in a spout of streaming water and collapsed across the upper edge. Sterling draped a towel over her heaving shoulders.

"Dry off; you'll feel better in a moment. I'm sorry, but Arcad was a little too stubborn."

"Kam," Arcad mumbled from the floor.

"Still in the grip of those tender emotions." Sterling shook his head. "Since you're such a singular individual, you might not know that people don't waste feelings when they're not returned. And Kam was very angry with you on the way in. She said you almost killed me—and you did, you know. I wasn't prepared even for your disorganized interruption. Even though it ended up convincing the governor. Surprising how violently hate can build."

Kam came over. She seemed to have recovered her breath. Without a change in expression she reached back and slapped Arcad full in the face. In his drugged condition, the blow stunned him momentarily.

"Well done!" Sterling clapped. "But it's never the blow that really hurts. Show what you think, baby."

Her face twisted. What in God's name was he doing to her? He tried funneling his energy, reaching out to stop her, but nothing happened. He'd been stripped, for who knows how long. Then Kam spit at him; he held his breath, telling himself that it didn't matter, that the contempt on her face wasn't real. But the emotion was there. It was she. Her mind had been altered, and whether or not she really hated him made no difference at all.

"All right—" Sterling grabbed her wrist, preventing another strike. "This isn't that pleasant. I prefer the more mellow emotions. There's nothing better than watching young people in love, don't you agree? And you do love him, isn't that right, Kam?"

"Sterling!" Arcad yelled.

"Yes," she said, her voice breathy.

"Oh yes, you love Arcad, but there's no hope for it," said Sterling. "He's so lofty! Inaccessible. You've dreamed of him, and now at last you're close, but he refuses you. You try one last time. You offer everything you have, with all the power of your womanhood."

"Please, Ryan," she begged, her face gone soft and full. Bending low, with desire in her eyes, she unbuttoned his shirt to brush warm lips against his chest. "Love me, please." He couldn't look at her. The eyes were her eyes, open with need. Her lips parted, kissing his. Arcad closed his own eyes, fighting off the urge to surrender to her. To give in now would be the worst thing he'd ever done. But he couldn't contain his physical reactions. Sensing her success, she continued her caresses, until Arcad was hardly aware of Sterling tying his hands together with thin cord. First the thumbs, then middle fingers, last fingers, all with short, separate lengths. He finished quickly enough, bound Arcad's feet, then started working on Kam.

"Make her stop, Sterling! She doesn't want this."

"Oh, but you do. You know as well as I that she wants it too. At this moment. Lie together. Face to face, please. My wife and my rival—a lovely couple!"

Kam silently continued pushing her pubic bone against his.

"What are you going to do with us?"

"You'll be easier to get rid of this way," Sterling grunted, tying off the last knot.

"Then for God's sake give her her mind back."

The illusionist appeared surprised. "You want it the other way?"

"It would be better . . . than this."

Sterling halted on his way out. "Have it your way. Maybe it would be good for her to know what's going to happen. Well, don't say you didn't have your chance, Arcad. Too bad you didn't take it."

Then he left them—probably to get Rusty, Arcad thought. Kam stopped moving against him, though the smell of her was still heavy. He felt her tears on his neck.

"Kam, I'm sorry."

"Shut up!"

"I—"

Finally she seemed to get a fix on her surroundings, wiping her eyes on his shirt collar. It made him feel a little better. After a little while he spoke.

"What the hell happened?"

She sighed. "After . . . after he finished talking to Deliewe, he offered to take me home. I was still worried whether he was all right, and I was furious with you. Confused about the whole thing. So, I told him what we'd planned. He just seemed to go crazy after that."

"He still is. We're in trouble."

"Can you get your ropes off?"

"I couldn't scratch my own butt."

"I mean with . . ." she was uncomfortable with the idea, "you know."

"That's what I'm talking about. Somehow, your husband found out about parogen. It puts me out of commission."

"For how long?"

"Varies with the dose. Sometimes as long as twelve hours."

"By then we'll be fish food." She began rotating her shoulders. "He was in too big a hurry on me. I think I can just . . . there, uuh!" She held up her freed right hand proudly. "These others—"

"I've got a knife in my pocket."

"And I thought you were just glad to see me. Where is it?"

"Right side." He tried not to think about her hand forcing its way toward his pocket.

"Okay, got it." She pulled it out, clamped it in her teeth, and opened it. Quickly she cut her own bonds and started working on his. When free, Arcad sat up, moving his head in an effort to loosen his stiff neck—one of the effects of the parogen. Kam noticed his discomfort and helped out with a little massage.

"You know, that little bondage routine wasn't completely unpleasant."

He colored and turned away. "I didn't want it . . . not that way."

"Maybe we'll have another chance."

He looked at her curls, the way they hung down over her eyes. "I thought you hated me for sure when I left today."

"I did. For a while. I hadn't realized what I wanted before, and when I saw Al almost killed, I forgot all about how much I wanted to get free. I'm back now. Al's sick. Sick, and in control of all that power. He won't be able to stop himself."

"I know. And I can't stop him either. Not now, anyway. We've got to leave."

"No way. He'll just get stronger. We've got to fight. I've still got my hands!"

"I noticed."

"Shut up."

Arcad was thinking of Nukhulls. "Maybe we can scare your husband down. Here, where's the rest of that rope?"

"Right here. Why?"

"Hands, please. We're going to make him think we're still

tied together. That, and a little misdirection." He tied her hands in a loose approximation of the original bonds, and then simulated the loops around knees, waist, and neck that had bound them tightly together. With the three meters or so left, Arcad fashioned a noose, slipping it over the head of the wax Houdini. Then, standing on the pallet of silver, he threaded the free end over a light fixture, tying the end to the knob of the closed door.

"Oh," she smiled, "I'm getting it."

"Right. Hunch over to the wall there. He'll probably have a looksee before he opens the door right away. I'll be behind, with this." He hefted the gold bar he had made, which was a little too heavy for a satisfactory weapon. I'll have to hold back, he thought, so I don't crush his skull. . . .

The sound of footsteps came from outside the door.

"Arcad?"

"Shh!"

"Listen. If I get up, I want you to step back and be quiet, okay?"

"What—"

"Promise me!"

Sterling tried the door, halted, then pushed through, drawing the line taut. The wax effigy lifted from its stand and swung from the fixture, its neck bent; snapped; hung.

"Harry!" he shrieked. *"Harry!"* Sterling sprang atop the silver, embracing his ikon. Arcad waited, then lunged, tackling Sterling to the ground. They struggled; Arcad got a handful of Sterling's hair, yanking his head back for a backhand slap to the face. He went for the choke hold, but Sterling was too quick for him. With a streetfighter's moves he threw off his opponent, immobilizing him with a quick shot to the groin. Breathing heavily, he stood over the woozy Arcad.

"And now, you sonofabitch—"

Kam lurched to her feet. There was a look of total disorientation on her face. "Al . . ." her voice croaked, "he's got . . . me, help—"

Sterling whirled. "What—"

It was what Arcad needed. With all his strength he kicked Sterling squarely in the solar plexus. The man doubled over but did not fall. Arcad stood up, finishing him with a two-fisted smash to the face. Sterling hung for a moment, pinned to the air like a specimen. Then he collapsed.

"Come on!" Kam grabbed Arcad's hand, pulling him through the museum and into the elevator. There, Arcad leaned against the side of the car to catch his breath.

"Nice work."

"I've been onstage for twenty years too," she said bitterly. "He should have remembered that."

"So should I." They got off on the top level. "What next?"

"He won't be out long."

"Then we'd better get out, fast."

"No way."

"Kam, we can't fight him now. Maybe we can surprise him again, but knocking him out doesn't do any good. We've got to wait until I get my stuff back."

"Go if you want, I'm not leaving. I'll handle him as best I can."

"That doesn't make sense!"

"And neither do you! Stop fooling yourself, for chrissakes, Arcad."

"I'm not—"

"Then dammit, do what you were sent here to do."

He tried touching her, but she'd already turned away. "All right. That's what you want, that's what you'll get. You have any amphetamines around here?"

"Some diet pills, I think, old ones. Why?"

"Never mind, just get 'em." He followed her to the bathroom, where Kam searched through dozens of vials and bottles in the medicine chest. Finally she found what she was looking for and handed it to Arcad. He shook the bottle. Six tiny pills. He had no idea if it would be enough. Kam filled a cup with water.

"Not that way, too slow. Here." He dumped the pills onto the ceramic top of the toilet tank, and then, with the bottom of the cup, crushed the drug into a fine powder. Pinching the product between thumb and forefinger, he sniffed all of it up. His sinuses burned; Arcad bent down low to catch his breath, to keep from sneezing. Already he felt light-headed, but there was no response yet from his center of power. It was still contained, thoroughly glazed over.

But starting to melt slightly.

"Kam, go down to the beach."

"It's raining like crazy out there. I'm staying."

He wanted to change her mind, but decided against risking using the energy. His power was coming back—but how much?

"Then promise me you'll stay out of the way unless I get in trouble. This is something I have to do. You said so yourself."

"All right." She smiled the smile he thought he would never see again. "I want you to know something, though."

"What's that?"

"We will get that chance we were talking about."

This time he kissed her, even though he knew it couldn't be genuine. Not with her. She brushed his cheek, went into her bedroom, and shut the door. Arcad found the lights for the hallway. He stood waiting in the darkness, thinking of his mother.

Mother, I'm sorry, he thought. He imagined her kind face, sensed the strong warmth in her arms. I'm sorry you thought you had to cure me. I couldn't let you destroy me, I was only trying to show you. . . .

Somehow, the guilt didn't feel the same anymore. Maybe it corresponded to his own level of power, or maybe things hadn't happened that way after all. He was too confused to sort out anything now. He heard the elevator stop, and as its door opened . . .

The sound of a shot boomed off the concrete walls. Too late, Arcad tried seizing hold of the projectile and was blasted against the wall. The lights came on. Sterling stood over him, holding the chrome .45 from the party. Arcad blinked his eyes.

"What the—"

Bits of twisted circuitry stuck out through the hole in Arcad's shirt. The bullet had struck Nukhulls' Finder! Arcad wasted no time knocking the gun away. He hooked his leg behind Sterling's and gave him a quick push to the floor. Sprawled on his back, the illusionist still managed a sneer.

"Harry's very angry, Arcad, do you know that?"

"I don't give a damn."

"At you and at Kam. Oh, I know where she is. Come out, dear." She walked out as commanded, her face a study in singular composure.

"It's me you want. Let her go!"

"I noticed you don't hesitate using her when it suits you."

"Don't you have any respect for her?"

He got to his feet. "I don't have to respect anyone."

"Yes. Yes you do." Arcad closed his eyes. The power was there—weak, but there. He turned as fine an edge as he could, slicing through Sterling's wide-band compulsion to grip Kam's mind. As she stiffly turned toward him, he saw the light of approval in her eyes. She would be the pawn—if it would help.

He felt the energy of Sterling's projections increase and tried balancing it. For a dark, weightless moment, the forces canceled each other out. Then Kam broke free, running past Arcad to the stairway behind him.

"Let her go, Sterling."

"Perhaps you're right. First things first. I'll get to her eventually." Arcad tried freezing him where he stood, but Sterling quickly broke through.

"It's wrong, Sterling. Don't you see what a waste this is?"

"On the contrary—ah, Rusty—"

When Arcad turned, it was he who was paralyzed. Rusty wasn't there. Sterling casually walked past.

"I'll see you later. Chin up." Then he went down the stairs after his wife. Gradually the paralyzing energy ceased, leaving Arcad nauseated and weak, unable to think of a way to beat the crazed magician. But the thought of Kam out there alone with him was enough to drive the doubt from his mind. He followed the stairs to the second floor, and saw that the steel doorway was open to the driving storm and all the outside lights were on. Out into the cold he went—into a wind that nearly blew him from the landing.

"Kam!"

No answer. He looked up. She was on top of the observation platform, kicking at Sterling's hands as he tried scaling the last few rungs of the ladder. Suddenly she was knocked back, as if pushed by a huge, invisible hand. Arcad ran to the base of the ladder. Cypress branches whipped against his face and his seriously bruised chest. He could hear nothing but the wind and the crashing waves.

The blue lights illuminating the oceanside rocks had also been turned on. He went up and saw Kam lying against the railing, apparently unconscious.

"Come for the execution, eh," Sterling screamed. "Get up for the witness, my dear!"

She jerked up like a rag doll hooked to a fishing line.

"No!" Arcad was able to hold her where she was.

"Go on." Sterling laughed. "It won't do you any good." He wheeled her toward the edge of the platform, making her turn so fast that her arms swung straight out, like those on a steam engine governor. As Arcad grabbed for her once more, he noticed a strange look of anticipation play Houdini's face. With all he had left, he enveloped Kam with a protective field, at the same time pushing against the force he estimated Sterling was exerting.

When that force cut off abruptly, Kam flew over the edge to disappear in the darkness.

Sterling ran to where she'd fallen. "What did you do!"

"Me? It was you—"

"You've killed her!" Sterling sobbed as he fell to his knees. Arcad did not waste the opportunity. His mind blazed with the frustration, guilt, and humiliation Sterling had caused him. He blasted it away. Sterling turned. There was hatred, a rush of confusion, the recognition that he had miscalculated. He stiffened, grunting in surprise.

"Now—" He was doing it. At last, he was doing it! His soul expanded, directing pure energy that sought out the source of his rival's power, burning it away, every trace of it.

"You are—Sterling—a punk from Chicago—a fake—a murderer—" Arcad stood over him. The blue eyes were open to the rain that blasted down. His jaw was slack, all muscles relaxed.

"You don't have it, you don't remember how you got it, you will never, ever be able to use it again. Tell me!"

"Y-y—"

"Tell me!"

"Yes yes yes yes yes yes yes yes yes yes—"

Mother broke in: Stop, son. Don't kill him. It was her voice, whispering happily to him. But Arcad didn't want to listen now.

He cut off all the lights.

He calmed the sea where he thought she had fallen.

Then he turned, and without looking at the Great Houdini went down to the pad and stole the magician's hopper.

10.

Nearly five full months later, on July Fourth:

Nukhulls sat alone in his control van, stashed in an alley off Bush Street in downtown San Metro. Directly over his chair was a video monitor which relayed the scene in nearby Union Square. An ironic name for the park, considering what was about to happen there. It was packed with people; they had taken over the street, and were clinging to lampposts or sitting perched on the awnings and cornices of the building surrounding the square. The entire facade, in fact, of the venerable Saint Francis Hotel appeared to be in the control of swarms of human flies. And the only break in the sea of humanity were the traveler palms and stately junipers lining the Post and Geary sides of the park. These had not been scaled because they were just too prickly.

In the center of all this was the gray column commemorating a long-forgotten war with the Spanish. The column no longer terminated in a Victory bearing trident and wreath, however. Now there were three primary lasers which would project Houdini's space illusion in brilliant three-D; these, along with the power cables, the cooling vanes, and the cherry picker, which was carrying technicians to make the last-minute adjustments which would assure that the video from orbit would be sharp and bright.

That signal passed first through the equipment in Nukhulls' van. By hitting any of a row of toggles, he could get a different city on his monitor. Atlanta. D.C. Saint Paul. All of them broadcasting outdoors, with their signals being fed from the equipment in front of him.

Then there were the millions of home sets. These got the feed from Nukhulls also, through their local broadcasting stations. This arrangement had upset some of the technical people connected with the July Fourth Committee, but Nukhulls had stood his ground against their petty obstructions and won out. So what if an extra relay satellite would have to come on line? He wanted to control events from San Metro, from the adopted home of the Great Houdini. Here was contained the strongest seed of rebellion; here was where the tenuous Confederal Union would stand or be dissolved. If his sequence was effective here—if the rider signal generated Em pulses of sufficient strength (and none of the bench tests or the field trials had indicated otherwise)—then tomorrow Houseman would find himself in a good position indeed. A sociological and political depth charge had been prepared and primed. The easy delivery would be slipped in while Sterling went through with his demonstration of pap.

The next morning, support for secession, here and in the rest of the Confederation, would be reduced considerably. Perhaps Deliewe's own mind would be changed for him! It wasn't impossible. Nukhulls had felt the strength of Em during one of the tests, and it had made him feel hungry immediately after a heavy meal—all while watching a film on training Doberman pinschers. There wasn't any doubt that it would work. All he had to do was put the sequence program into his machine. His dish monitor on the panel would give him a three-D look at the proceedings as well as firsthand experience of the true force of the generated waves. Too much or too little at any particular time, and Nukhulls could override his own program by means of a rheostat mounted to the right of the dish. Em frequencies, in cycles per second, ran clockwise from the top: from beta, at 30–13 cps, corresponding to the wave pattern of an active, awake brain; alpha, at 12–8 cps, producing a state of passive awareness; then down to the two states capable of affecting his audience most powerfully—delta, from 7 to 4 cps, which imposed a wave pattern similar to that recorded during the long, dreamless intervals of sleep. And finally, the signal Nukhulls considered most effective, and most dangerous: theta, at 3 cps to 1 per second, the pattern produced during deepest sleep. Dreamtime, the one period where the subconscious was released—or could be most affected.

Further to the right on the panel was a little chrome joystick, which enabled him to retard or increase the framing and the development of his subliminal images—those of the threatening dragon. By twisting it, Nukhulls could modulate the *speed* of that image in frames per second. And by clicking it over to the side, he could alter its *intensity,* expressed on the scale around the control in percentages. Intensity was important in dealing with the visual threshold of a subject—the point at which he is able to recognize and comprehend an image flashed in his direction. In this case, the higher the percentage, the longer that the image—composed of flashes set to the desired framing speed—was actually onscreen within each individual second of viewing time. Thus, a 30 percent setting at a frame of 1:60 would be less likely to exceed the visual threshold than the same setting at a 1:1000 frame, simply because there would be less total flashes spread through each second of viewing time, with correspondingly longer intervals between each flash. The program Nukhulls had developed tied a gradual materialization of the image to violent shifts from feverish beta pulses to the deep, untenable booms of theta. These, of course, would accompany Sterling's overt peril as the illusionist's performance reached its peak.

Then, as tension was broken and all minds opened up by the Em—a simple message: unity; Houseman; security—and the emotions to back it up. Elegantly simple it was, and to those who might feel indignant about such meddling with the sainted "free will"—tough.

Tougher still to be forced into a civil war, to kill and possibly die themselves. Dead men, after all, have no voice in earthly affairs.

He put on his headset and checked his panel clock. Twelve-fifty. Ten minutes before the start of Sterling's segment. Through the vent atop the van he could hear swells of band music echoing off the buildings between himself and Union Square. Nukhulls smiled. Someone in the Regional Planning Commission—he suspected that it was Stassen—had exercised a veto to black out the rest of the broadcast. Nukhulls considered this stipulation sour grapes, a way for the commissioner from Fresno to save some face when the board had voted to allow the Sterling broadcast into the region. How could any sane person, he wondered, believe that an educated constituency would be swayed by a few smarmy political speeches? As usual, the fools had missed the real threat.

Nukhulls switched on his dish monitor, which showed the boom in orbit from camera sixteen. It hung motionless between the camera and the bright clouds of earth sixteen thousand kilometers below. The first cage was crowded with technicians working out a problem in the motor drive which was supposed to pull Houdini toward and through the molten silver. The actual metal had not yet been placed between the wound field paddles; netted tightly together, it had been tethered to the egress cage. A black target had been painted on one side of the cube to facilitate the melting process, which would be completed in less than ten minutes, according to the running schedule.

Sterling, of course, was nowhere to be seen. No doubt he was in the shuttle, meditating, praying for the skill needed to come through alive. Not that many prayers were needed. Houdini would be temporarily protected by a shroud of ablative material, long enough to survive the heat of the Passage. When

134

he emerged, his suit would be changed entirely to gold. A miracle!

More like a very expensive cheap trick.

According to Arcad, Sterling had intended to use that platform for a little compulsion of his own. But that had been changed, finally, once Arcad had become sufficiently motivated. Nukhulls only wished he knew more about what had happened that last night out on the Slide. According to news reports, Kam Sterling had committed suicide. Subsequently, Sterling himself had emerged from weeks of seclusion a changed man, a shell, with none of the old verve and daring—nothing, really, except a contractual commitment to perform today. There had been a halfhearted attempt to renege; a threatened lawsuit had put an end to that, thankfully, because Nukhulls had feared it would be necessary to go to Arcad once more.

And Arcad had disappeared. His Finder was dead. A check of the old house (where Nukhulls released George, much to the relief of both) showed it to still be in good repair, but with no sign of its former occupant. Nothing within a ten-kilo radius, either. Arcad might be in Australia, for all he knew, which might make things very inconvenient in the future. . . .

But, being a professional, Nukhulls wasn't overly concerned about that. Tomorrow he could begin the business of tracking down the psychokinetic. As for today, well, he could afford that feeling of satisfaction which comes when life's ironies can be appreciated fully. He remembered how Sterling had seemed such a formidable man, a deep well of mystery, impossible to deal with or predict. As for Arcad, how weak and flawed he'd been by his inability to accept his own nature.

And yet Arcad had won, defeating his blocks first, then brushing Sterling aside. Certainly the conditions might have been less than fair. But then, where were the illusionist's vaunted resourcefulness and guile, his strength of will and purportedly incomparable courage? Not to mention his own latent, developing psychokinetic abilities. Nukhulls glanced at the crowd on the screen. Most of these people were here to see their hero, the master escapologist. What they were going to see was Alphonse Sterling, a beaten fake, a tired huckster with an oversized parlor trick. Who would ever have thought it?

And no one knew it but him! Nukhulls noticed that his ready light was on, indicating that the satellite feed through his equipment could commence. Smiling, he activated the system, listening with pleasure to the cooling fans as they kicked on. It was T plus five minutes, time to check wave strength and synchronize it properly with the incoming signal. Reaching to his left, he switched on a remote microphone mounted atop the Victory column beneath the radiating vanes. The blast of music startled him, so he eased the volume down while noting that two of the three VU meters jumped smartly. The third would indicate the level of subliminal hum. This test involved the production of an Em pulse in the beta of thirty-five cps, which, if generated at a proper strength, would produce an audible, involuntary vocal response from anyone within wave range. His target was a decibel level of −5, and the VU meter had been marked accordingly with a line from a black felt-tip pen.

β **Em 35 cps**
frame 0:0

"Okay," he whispered, "hum key on . . . mark." He started the rider generator, modulating the pulses with his joystick. Intensity adjustment was achieved by twisting the ring at the butt of the stick swivel. The third meter moved: −20, −12, 7, 6, 6 again, −5.

He could hear it, something like the drone of Coptic priests reconsecrating the limestone gallery of the pyramid of Cheops at Giza. Nukhulls watched the meters, and when he was satisfied that the level was holding, he screwed the lock cap tightly onto the ring. The rider signal was shunted to a pause status; he was ready. The predetermined conclusion might almost be considered a disappointment.

Nukhulls sat back. The depression would come, certainly. But there was other work, new projects. Perhaps a vacation first. Canada was a nice, sane place to visit, as long as one stayed away from the Quebec frontier.

Someone knocked on the door of the van. Had Duenos found him? And what the hell had happened to the plainclothes guards who were supposed to keep the strays off. . . .

No screw-ups now, he thought. Not now.

He went to the door and opened it. Standing on the step was a tall man, tan, wearing sunglasses and a tattered leather jacket. The man smiled. His hair was white as fine china.

"Hello, Bruce," he said.

"Arcad! Jesus Christ, get in here!"

When he stepped up, the two men stood looking at each other. Finally, Nukhulls extended his hand.

"I didn't get a chance to thank you last time."

Arcad removed his glasses, revealing eyes that were more baked than they had ever been. He blinked for a few moments before he noticed what Nukhulls was doing. They shook hands with emphasis, if not with warmth.

"You don't have to thank me. Orders, remember?"

"Well, sit down, for chrissakes." Nukhulls kicked a stool over, but the big man remained standing. "Where've you been?"

"The desert. Taos region."

"Doing what, besides getting fried?"

"Walking a lot. Thinking. Went to the mountains to try survival. Then back to the desert."

Nukhulls remembered his board. Two minutes, everything still go. "Man," he said, "you don't know how glad I am to see you. I couldn't get your signal."

"Your Finder came in handy." Arcad suddenly unbuttoned his shirt to reveal the scar tissue on his chest. "Your box stopped a bullet for me. Now it's slightly out of commission." He looked up at the Union Square monitor. "Have you been out there?"

"I'm not too fond of crowds like that."

"It's insane. Absolutely crazy. People running around, slamming into each other, people punching, people kissing. Like the end of the war." He tossed Nukhulls a piece of candy wrapped in cellophane. "Have some—"

"They printed his face on it, huh?"

"The candy sucks. More a souvenir, I think."

Nukhulls chewed on the stale taffy. "So tell me how it was so easy to find *me*."

"Time tells in the mountains. I can read a little better than before."

"Listen, I'm a little busy right now. Why don't you come back in a half hour—" He glanced uselessly at Arcad in an attempt to fathom anything in those alkali eyes. But Arcad only sat down without a word.

Oh hell, Nukhulls thought. Slowly, he slid the switch on his belt, activating the laser of his dead-man. As a precaution. But there wasn't time to consider the situation any further, because the three-D image popped suddenly onto the dish monitor. The time was exactly 1:00 P.M. WDT, July 4, 2079. The first shot was a straight-on horizontal of the boom, clear of crew now, from the white concrete of the countermass to the cages lined together at the opposite end. Still netted together, the cube of silver had been towed into the paddle field, where it remained, solidly suspended. The metal reflected ambient light too strongly, but that only added to the spectacular appearance of the prop. The crowd in the square saw the same shot, with the countermass seemingly pivoting over the column. The crowd saw the illusion as if they were above it—meaning that whenever the overhead cameras were used, earth seemed to be hanging just twenty-five meters above the street. It was an intimidating perspective for some, who crouched, smiling nervously, but crouching all the same.

"That's an excellent picture, Nukhulls."

A roll of drums rattled windows for blocks around, then:

"From synchronous orbit twelve thousand kilometers above Washington, D.C., it's the Great Houdini! Good afternoon, ladies and gentlemen. I'm Brian Stacey, in orbit with the Houdini party to bring what

I'm certain will be a tremendously exciting event to you on this three-hundred and third anniver—" A lapse of static indicated the regional censorship, to which the multitude responded with a hearty cheer.

"Shit," Nukhulls murmured.

"A little touchy out there, aren't they?"

"Not for long—" he began, and then halted, with the realization that it might be a mistake to boast to the man seated behind him. The announcer broke for a beer commercial.

"That's an interesting setup," Arcad said, staring at Nukhulls' controls.

"It's the end result of our last project. Think of it as an experiment in political motivation." Nukhulls suddenly was too nervous to concentrate. Arcad had changed, and seemed immune to the old leverage Nukhulls had always successfully applied. The string of sponsored messages completed itself.

"We're back now, as the last of Houdini's crew leaves the boom. The figures you will see floating in from your right—yes, there they are—are part of an inspection committee, which Houdini always insists upon when he performs any of his larger stage escapes. He doesn't want a doubt in anyone's mind that the danger to himself isn't real, or that there's trickery involved. Doubly important, as you understand, when the bulk of the audience is so far removed—"

"Boom looks a little different up there, doesn't it?"

Arcad shrugged. "Not really."

Great. He won't be distracted.

"All right, I understand the inspection team has radioed their report to the man I have with me right now, Dr. Glen Wright of NEIT. Doctor, welcome."

"Thank you, Brian."

"I wonder if you would mind, first of all, briefly describing how this illusion will work."

"Well. In about three minutes, Houdini's crew will activate the lasers which will melt the silver. After that process is completed, the boom will be set in motion, by which time Houdini will have been tied and attached to the pulley line, to be pulled from the first cage toward the silver, a distance of perhaps five meters."

"I see. How long will it then take for him to reach the silver, once he's out of the cage?"

"Two minutes exactly."

"Not much time."

"No. And I thought it would be interesting to show the gloves he'll be wearing as he attempts to untie those knots." The doctor displayed a pair of silver gloves which did not appear to be very flexible. "Now, these rely on their own elastic compression rather than on air pressure, which means they're thinner than the standard suit gloves worn by the technicians, for example. Even so, it will still be a difficult business for him to extricate himself in time."

"Okay. Can you summarize the report of your crew?"

"I'd be happy to. They thoroughly checked the laser system, the silver it- self—"

"How much silver is that, by the way?"

"Just short of sixty-five metric tons—or fifty million dollars' worth, if you prefer to think of it that way."

"If I had that kind of money lying around I'd take a vacation."

Dr. Wright smiled. "Well, Houdini has said that there is no better way for him to relax than this. But, if I can finish, spe- cial attention was paid to the asbestos ropes which will be used to tie him, and to the pulley system itself. Everything is perfectly in order and functional. We could find no evidence at all of any hidden mechanism."

"So it is your committee's finding that everything is in order and perfectly legitimate."

"Yes. We will be filing a sworn statement to that effect with the solicitor general's office in the morning."

"Okay. Thank you very much, Dr. Glenn Wright. We'll be back in a moment!"

The orbit shot dissolved to a shot of a grinning workman who extolled the virtues of a new line of "effortless" spanners. Nuk- hulls sat back in his chair, swiveling delib- erately toward his erstwhile partner. But it was Arcad who spoke first.

"Well, Nukhulls, this should be a big day for you."

"Just like all the rest."

Arcad stared off at nothing. "I'm a little sad myself."

"For him?"

"Not him. He got what he deserved. For a while I didn't think so. I blamed you for what happened. But then I realized that you were right, he had to be stopped, not only for what he might do now, but for later. And I was the one to stop him."

"And you did. What's with the curiosity now? Why'd you come back here?"

"To see what he had left. I almost killed him out there that night."

"Because of Kam."

"Yeah." He rubbed his eyes. "But I knew that what happened wasn't really his fault either. She couldn't settle on what she wanted. Old excitement or new excitement. Sterling or me. And she waited too long to choose the winning side—" He broke off, shaking his head.

"Hey, you did your job. You should be proud."

"The job isn't finished yet."

"Hello again, everybody. I've just been informed that, yes, they are about to fire the lasers. There they go!"

Twin blue beams flicked on target; gradually, individual ingots lost definition. The netting burned away as the edges of the cube softened. A dark swirl of slag came to the surface, drawn by increasing convection.

"What do you mean, Arcad—"

"There's you." The psychokinetic spread his arms. "This."

"And what the hell's that mean!" Nukhulls was angry now.

"Have you ever been alone? I'm not talking about spending the night alone by choice. I mean having no one. And no chance. It's not an entirely pleasant experience."

"You made that choice for yourself."

"No. This wasn't for me to decide. Even now I'm alone. But until I went to Taos I hadn't really felt what that meant, how precious a thing it is to rely on yourself. The ability to choose suddenly becomes very important. Most people don't know. Most of 'em are satisfied doing what other people tell them to do."

The silver had become a globe, obviously liquid, wobbling slightly on twin pillars of light. There was silence, and a three-quarters elevated shot of the boom.

"And now, ladies and gentlemen: the Great Houdini!"

Two suited figures, one of them Houdini, in a silver pressure suit trimmed in black—the other, the man who would tie him—entered the camera field from the left. Both got into the cage; Nukhulls heard the cheers of the crowd through his speaker and, with a slight lag, from the open vent.

"It occurred to me," Arcad said, oblivious to the appearance of the man he had defeated, "that you were going to do exactly what I prevented Sterling from doing."

A camera pulled in close on Houdini's helmet. Inside, he was smiling, eyes bright, wavy hair impeccably smoothed. He waved in response to the greeting he heard through his earplug monitor, being careful to turn in all the proper directions. Obviously, he had the camera angles studied well.

Nukhulls stood up and drew his crystal, leveling it at Arcad.

"I'll kill you if you make a move."

He felt the tingling at the back of his skull. . . .

"Don't forget the dead-man, either!"

The buzz faded. Still facing Arcad, Nukhulls put the sequence tape into the console with his free hand. Licking his lips, he released the pause control.

δ Em 10
frame 1:200
20%

"No one's getting hurt. Nice and easy in the start." He felt the pulses himself, and saw Arcad relax slightly.

Houdini's voice came over slightly nasal from his suit mike: "Thank you, folks, thank you very much. My friend here is going to be tying me in a strange way, so I hope you won't mind a few guttural noises while he's doing it."

"Tell me what gives you the right, Nukhulls!"

"Rights!" Nukhulls waved the crystal. "I'll shoot you if you don't stay down! What makes you, of all people, think there is such a thing as rights? You think that air gives you the right to breathe? You've got to fight, you come out screaming and take what you can. That's right. I'm saving lives with this and— Ah, what's the use! Just keep your mouth shut, or so help me, I don't care what I promised your mother—"

"What!"

Houdini's assistant looped a cord around

each of the illusionist's ankles. Then, from brackets along the inside corner of the cage, the assistant removed a metal bar. Houdini placed his hands behind his back, clamping the bar against his chest with his elbows. His wrists were then tightly bound, which effectively immobilized Houdini's entire upper torso.

"Watch it, my friend, I'm not made of rubber."

δ **Em 4 cps**
frame 1:1200
60%

A surge of fear here was just right; Nukhulls gripped the Em control between thumb and forefinger. Otherwise, the subliminal framing was just right.

"I'm talking to you, Nukhulls! What do you know about her?"

"God damn it, there isn't time now!"

Arcad looked devastated. "I didn't kill her, did I—"

"Don't be shy," Houdini quipped. "Truss

δ **Em 5 cps**
frame 1:1000
49%

me, you fool—uumph! A little more, that's it." With a pull of a slip knot, the assistant brought Houdini's hands and feet together. His back arched impossibly. A little more delta increased the feeling of closeness in the van; then, back up to beta, so that everyone could think about what was going to happen. Like a pig ready for the spit, Sterling floated inside the cage while the other man attached to the line a meter-square cube of flesh-colored plastic. He pressed the large red button which initiated the cycle. The cube started toward the silver.

"All these years," Arcad whispered hoarsely. "You've played on that all these years—"

β **Em 29 cps**
frame 1:375
40%

"That, friends, is an organic plastic which approximates the density and mass of my own body. In a moment you'll be able to see what the heat of that metal will do to it—and to me, should I fail."

β Em 18 cps
frame 1:300
25%

Determining that everything was following schedule, Nukhulls allowed the preset program to continue. The plastic hit the silver and was swallowed by it. Immediately, surface tension of the sterling globe was shattered by eruptions of vaporized solid, which threw off coin-size beads of silver in an expanding halo surrounding the boom. Even though Nukhulls realized that the "test" was a ruse, that the plastic cube was expanding at this moment to form the shroud that would protect Sterling, he still felt the dread produced by the combination of Em waves and image. On some of the slower frames, he got a clear impression of yellow, slit-pupil eyes. It was impossible to separate the dual emotional currents, one artificial and onscreen, the other here and very real.

"You were supposed to be my friend!"

"I'm not telling you again!" Arcad appeared rocked by the vibrations of the roaring crowd. They were physically shaking the pavement—there was his response at last! A fist-size knot of glazed ash appeared in the egress cage. The program backed off. . . .

α Em 8 cps
frame 1:300
10%

"Reminds you of some of those great home-cooked meals, eh, folks?" Houdini quipped. "Barbequed mylar." The camera panned back to a full-boom image. Nukhulls winced under the effects of the last

147

theta surge. He had used it sparingly, since it was capable of producing a deep and lasting psychosis.

"Get out of here, Arcad."

"No." It was a standoff.

Tied as he was, Houdini had difficulty breathing. Then again, he might be faking to make a better show of it. "All right, pal," he said at last, "hook me up!"

By means of a toggle and clamp, he was fastened to the pulley line. The assistant checked the bonds and the connection, then floated out of the cage.

All right, set 'em up!

β **Em 29 cps**
frame 1:750
45%

Nukhulls increased the programmed strength by a full third, just enough to give everyone a nice jolt. Houdini was alone but his voice boomed off a thousand windows:

"Whew! If ever I felt tied down by my job, it's now. Seriously, though, before I start I'd like to say that in the twenty years I've been performing I've never had such a response. Thank you all."

Now the cheers were a little uncertain. Sterling was penciled for a thirty-second speech here, but it was becoming clear that the schedule wouldn't be followed. There was the risk of breaking the mood, but Nukhulls halted the sequence temporarily. It would not do to abandon the precise synchronization of event and pulse.

Houdini nodded his appreciation as best he could. "Thanks. You know, I've learned a few things the last couple of years, and one of the most important is that presentation is more eloquent than any verbal description can be. The masters of the past advise one to perform and not to lecture. I usually try following that very sensible admonition.

"Today, however, is special, and I must break that rule. For this, dear friends, will be my last illusion. I'm retiring from the stage, and accordingly take advantage of the fitting opportunity—this being the anniversary of our nation's founding—to thank some of the people who have helped so much over the years."

"What the hell—" Nukhulls looked at Arcad accusingly, but the psychokinetic wasn't even looking at the monitor. There was impatient movement along the edges of the crowd; to compensate, Nukhulls set up a steady pulse designed to increase expectation.

α Em 10 cps
frame 1:1800
70%

"First of all, I must give credit to the wonderful woman who helped design this piece of equipment, as well as many of the other effects which have been so successful and entertaining to all of you. Unfortunately . . ."

Sterling's voice broke; Arcad looked up as if he'd just been able to sort out everything.

"Unfortunately, she can't be here today. But I love you, Kam, wherever you are right now. As for others—the crew topside with me, as well as the support people on the ground, have been simply outstanding. I appreciate the efforts all of you have made.

"But, to the main point: Some of the history students out there are aware that my name—my stage name, at least—is not original. The name Houdini has been used before. One hundred fifty years ago, Ehrich Weiss, Mr. Harry Houdini, practiced our mutual art to the acclaim of the entire world. For almost forty years he performed across the continents, earning the praise and adoration of an age more youthful than our own. He never let his fame control him. True, he had a temper, but he did not allow it to interfere with his craft. Incredibly enough, he was basically a shy man, considerate and honorable, devoted to his wife Bess. Characteristics which, I'm afraid to say, are opposite those usually required to attain the level of fame and prestige this man had.

"Yet, everything he gained was by the effort of his own will and imagination. He was the ultimate showman, and by taking his name I hoped in some small way to pay tribute to his memory." Houdini paused for a few moments to catch his breath.

"You know, Harry's philosophy was simple. He realized that a successful performer prevails not by bludgeoning his audience but by guiding it, arranging his effects in a way that makes the audience *want* to believe in what he is doing, in what seems patently impossible. Without boasting, I think I can truthfully say that I have never tried to force an audience, and that my own success is based on what is really a kind of consideration.

"I'd like you all to think about the consequences of force, friends, as you watch what I'm about to do, and think about the difference between compulsion and persuasion. Meanwhile, I dedicate this Passage Through Molten Silver to Mr. Harry Houdini. And I pray that when it's over, you'll understand what I mean when I say: 'I am not the other Houdini!' Rockets!"

Verniers on the right of Sterling's cage flicked out. Slowly, the boom began moving, sweeping the air above the multitude at Union Square. This was it! Nukhulls restarted the program. The tension had to build now almost to the breaking point, with delta like a blow to the stomach.

θ **Em 1**
frame 1:1500
60%

From orbit: "And now, ladies and gentlemen, the test! One! Two! Three!" And with a quick movement of his head, Houdini touched the button which started him out of the cage and toward the silver. He was almost halfway there before he even moved, but suddenly he began pivoting his shoulders forward violently. The bar came away from his chest, flashing away through the light and harsh shadows. Meanwhile,

β **Em 30**
frame 1:1750
60%

taking advantage of the slack thus provided, Houdini drew his knees up far enough to enable him to bring his bound wrists and ankles around in front of him. Nukhulls felt his ears ring when fourth- and fifth-wave harmonics kicked in. The dragon's face was now almost completely

β **Em 30/720**
frame 1:1820
83%

formed, the Chinese terror accompanying the slow inching of the illusionist toward metallic agony.

151

Arcad moaned. "No . . . it's all wrong!" Rising like a bronze colossus, he reached toward Nukhulls' panel. Nukhulls pushed him away, then felt his mind slipping away as Arcad commenced a mental assault. Too late, Nukhulls tried to warn him; but, with a tiny click echoing far in the reaches of his head, the dead-man lashed out. Arcad fell with a scream, shot in the knee, and Nukhulls quickly switched off the weapon. A roar came from the crowd. Houdini had freed his left foot and his right hand. A bare meter from the silver, both hands came up in the harsh sunlight as he worked on the final knot.

Yet his motion wasn't frantic, it was deliberate, though he had to be feeling the heat. Nukhulls' panel began to smoke. *Arcad!*

β **Em 30/2160**
frame 1:1900
85%

θ **Em 1**
frame 1:2000
100%

"Stop it!" He whirled and kicked Arcad full in the face, smashing the fiery nostrils, bursting those burning yellow eyes. He got back to the panel, gripped the stick. . . .

Sterling couldn't do it! The limb of the silver sphere reached for him, and he was engulfed, with arms desperately spread, fists clenched. The suit mike was off but the mouth was a chasm of pain. The theta was like the soulless boom of a universal organ, threatening to rattle all substance apart, atom by atom . . .

And then he was gone. Arcad stirred, bleeding from the nose. The crowd in Union Square was absolutely silent, unable to deal with the reality of Houdini's failure.

152

Quickly, Nukhulls checked the timer. Twenty seconds until the clincher, until the miracle, scheduled to save everyone just as the impression of death was grasped. The pulses cut, the image faded.

The dish monitor in front of him exploded.

"Arcad, no!" he screamed. "They'll go nuts!"

"You're lying—"

Plastic melted, filling the van with foul black smoke.

"Look at them. Look! You've got to let it finish!"

Arcad hesitated. Fifteen seconds, sixteen, seventeen—Houdini should be reappearing right now. . . . Along with the new image

HOUSEMAN

δ **Em 6**
frame 1:350
90%

which did come. But there was no Houdini. All that emerged was a charred lump the size of a basketball. Somehow, in spite of the fire, the program was still running, uncontrolled:

HOUSEMAN
HOUSEMAN
HOUSEMAN
HOUSEMAN
HOUSEMAN

Tension was still being generated at unbearable levels. Barely able to breathe,

Nukhulls grabbed at his control stick, but it burned his fingers. The entire panel was fused anyway.

δ **Em 6**
frame 1:350
90%

"You fool!" Nukhulls screamed. "He's dead!"

He saw the crowd breaking up, crazed by the death of their hero, at the sight of his remains circling again and again at the end of the boom. Shielding his face, Nukhulls kicked open the van door and staggered out into the alley, where he was assaulted by an overwhelming impression of

HOUSEMAN.

Arcad was still inside. Nukhulls went back in and dragged Arcad out on his back. Already, parts of the mob were running past on Bush Street. There was the smell of more smoke, and the sound of glass breaking.

"Arcad, come on—"

"I can't walk."

"Lean on my shoulder. Let's go—that van's loaded with fuel!" He pulled Arcad along. Someone bumped into them and he thrashed out with his free arm.

"You know this town. Where the hell can we get away from this?"

"The park . . . Oooph. Yerba Buena. A few blocks south of here. Let me fix . . . my knee—"

"No time—"

"I have to rest." Arcad slumped against the side of a jewelry store.

"Come on, here's another alley." They pushed their way through knots of people, many of whom were half insane. In front of them, a screaming old man pounded mercilessly on the back of a pregnant woman. Others walked aimlessly, bumping into parked vehicles and street signs. At the mouth of the alleyway they got a clear view of Union Square, with the

154

boom swinging like a sickle atop the column. At least thirty people had scaled it, some of whom were hanging from the loose cables. The image flickered, but held, punctuated by

HOUSEMAN.

"Jesus Christ," he whispered. Now Nukhulls pushed him into the alley, which looked deserted. At the far end was parked an empty hopper.

"All right, let's go!" Arcad followed as best he could, dragging his maimed leg behind him. Nukhulls popped the bubble, hot-wired the inductor ignition, then jumped out again to help his partner in. It took too long. Before he could get back into the pilot's seat, he saw a crystal pointed at his eyes, a bare six centimeters between them.

"Turn it off!" said a familiar voice.

Nukhulls looked up.

"Duenos!"

"Bruce!" The senator was genuinely pleased. "And your long-lost friend, I see."

"Let's get back to the compound—"

"A splendid suggestion. Into the back with you." Duenos still had not lowered his weapon.

"What is this?"

"I'm afraid both of you are under arrest."

Nukhulls didn't move, and the senator's smile faded.

"Please cooperate. I'm perfectly willing to kill you at the moment. And I'll take that crystal in your pocket. Slowly, that's it."

Stunned, Nukhulls handed his weapon over before releasing the controls and crawling to the back as ordered. Duenos got in, closing the bubble. His expression was a mixture of horror and excitement, a fascination at seeing this fission of political bonds. Wasteful, but at the same time compelling. The quiet whir seemed impossible as they lifted off.

"For the love of God, Bruce, what have you been doing?"

"I—" And then Nukhulls stopped as they rose above Union Square. The boom flickered madly now, and finally went out. All that remained was the single word in red:

HOUSEMAN

hanging above the howling beast of a mob in the center of San Metro.

11.

The dispensary at Santa Cruz Compound had been converted
to a holding cell for the two prisoners. Arcad's knee was at-
tended to—burned cartilage and flesh excised, the bone being
patched with a kind of resin paste—while Nukhulls was given
a heavy shot of tranquilizers to counteract the effects of nervous exhaustion. Bars were mounted on the windows, with a
guard placed at each of the three triple-locked doors.

Arcad received a shot of parogen every six hours.

After a day or so Nukhulls felt recovered. The old energy
returned, but his only release was pacing around the six empty
beds—all that remained of medical equipment in the building.
Everything else, down to tongue depressors and tape, had been
taken away.

So Nukhulls paced, and thought of what had happened, what
had gone wrong. There was a seventh bed in the room. Arcad
lay on it, sleeping most of the time, staring listlessly whenever
he did wake up. He was like the long-term comatose patient
who sits up suddenly to blink, seems to look around at the
relative who might be reading a magazine at the bedside, then
lies down again, lost. Nukhulls kept shaking him, getting no
response. It wasn't that Arcad couldn't see or hear, or couldn't
move because of the parogen. Perhaps he was unable to deal
with the events of the Fourth. Perhaps he felt responsible

for the incredible mayhem which had erupted in San Metro. God only knew why, but Ryan Arcad seemed to have taken the sins of man upon his shoulders. As though he could absorb them all and then die, leaving the world cleansed somehow.

Nukhulls, of course, cared nothing for such baroque doctrines. He felt no guilt. If anything, he felt that he had been prevented from accomplishing a very great and charitable work. The fault had been Sterling's, and only Sterling's. He remembered the illusionist's final admonition, that everyone think about compulsion and persuasion. Somehow, Sterling had known what was going to happen. Arcad had stripped him of his developing psychokinesis, but the old talents had been left intact, with devastating consequences. Nukhulls now realized that he was guilty of a technical miscalculation. He should never have constructed his plans so that a single unpredicted act could destroy them. He had been blinded, overcome by success, carried away.

But he knew his mistake now, and, knowing it, he was capable of self-correction. Next time there would be no such error.

The locks on the front door rattled open and a heavy orderly, followed by an armed guard, came in to inject Arcad with something. When the psychokinetic stirred, he was hauled to his feet and led out for what was likely to be another interrogation. It was pathetic, the way his crippled leg dragged.

"Hey, buddy," he called to the orderly, "why don't you give the guy a break?"

The orderly never even looked at him. Regional personnel, he reminded himself. The entire Confederal garrison had surrendered, without a fight, three hours after the broadcast.

So much for the future of the nation. He lay on the bed to wait for his own turn.

It was almost dark when they brought Arcad back. Nukhulls opened his eyes and saw him walking under his own power, still sluggish but seemingly more alert. He sat down on the bed next to Nukhulls', waiting for the orderly to lock up before saying anything.

"Well," Nukhulls said, "you look better."

"Don't feel that way." Arcad rubbed his eyes with the heels of both hands.

"Come on, how was it?"

"The captain and I had an interesting discussion."

"Really. He tell you what to do with this dinner?"

Arcad smiled, looking straight at Nukhulls as he said: "Washington had forwarded dossiers on us both."

Thrown to the wolves already. "And, being a friendly sort, the captain let you look at yours, eh?"

"I think he's trying to ingratiate himself."

"Did he succeed?"

"Ryan Allen Arcad, born 17 November, 2041."

"So he got your birth certificate."

"Father, Clarence Arcad, killed in action near Tsien Tung PROC, 9 August, 2036. I believe he was telling the truth."

Nukhulls jumped up and resumed his pacing. "How the hell can you believe something like that? Doesn't make sense—"

"You've got to tell me the truth!"

He sighed. "Do you actually think the truth will get you out of here? Because it sure as hell isn't going to make you happy."

"I'm tired of looking at you, knowing you've got part of my life tucked away."

"Ryan, we've always worked well together, wouldn't you say?"

"Yes."

"It's been satisfying, at least part of the time?"

"Yes. Sometimes, yes."

"And during those times you were happy, weren't you? You considered yourself my friend?"

Arcad did not answer. He sat, looking at the floor as if he were seeing through it.

"All right! You want it, I'll give it to you. I suppose you deserve that much. Your father first. He was a full colonel, army career officer. In accordance with wartime regulations, he had a sperm sample frozen and stored in a Washington sperm bank. Just like every other officer above second lieutenant. Shortly thereafter came the nuclear attack. It was meant as a show of force; they blew up the Washington Monument to start things off. Damage and casualties were light. No one knew that the residual radiation would have the effect it did."

"What do you mean?"

"Among other things, genetic alteration to the sperm at that particular bank. In the next ten years, six women including your mother had occasion to request insemination from that depository. There were four pregnancies. One set of mixed twins, and one girl—all three, normal. One stillbirth. And you. Ryan Arcad. An absolute terror by age three. Whenever you got angry, or hurt yourself . . . well, you know what you can do. That's when they started you on the parogen, but your mother couldn't stand what a large enough dose did to her baby. By the time you were four and a half, she'd had enough—"

"No!"

"Shut up, I'm finishing this. You were committed to the Penfield Research Hospital in Asheboro, North Carolina, where you remained until you were seventeen years old."

Arcad appeared lost. "I can't remember," he whispered, shaking his head.

"You wouldn't. They were pretty rough there, short of dissection. When they weren't running brain scans they had you on Quadrazine. You were a mess. After the first year, your mother stopped visiting you altogether. Didn't want to think about what was happening to her son. She's like you in that way."

"What about you, then?"

"I wasn't anxious to get my head shot off in China, so I opted for a stint with the Treasury Department. They paid for my education at night while I ran surveillance errands on the day shift. That seemed to be the coming thing. And then I got it into my head that I could actually use my new Ph.D. in experimental psychology. I took an assignment in

Asheboro, which is when I met you for the first time. I wrote out a therapy program—which stabilized you—and got a conservatorship, your mother being dead by this time. They released you into my protective custody. The first two years I spent rebuilding you from the ground up. Getting your 'problem' under control. Educating you. By then I'd moved to the Defense Department. I convinced my superiors that you would be useful for the kind of work thay had in mind for me. That's when you started living."

"I remember the apartment in Georgetown."

"Yep."

"I was big, and slim."

Now Nukhulls had to smile. "That's right—"

"And I was wanted for the murder of my mother—"

"Watch it! Hey, calm down. I don't know if the parogen will keep you from setting yourself off. Yeah, that's it." It was bad, on top of how bad everything else was, to see Arcad shaking like a newborn kitten. But the man was correct, he did have a right to know. Considering the circumstances, there was no longer any reason to keep anything from him.

"Nukhulls, what happened to her?"

"Before I tell you, I want you to think of something first— think about how normal people get a handle on themselves. People have to keep their behavior in check. Otherwise, no one would be able to get along. The planet couldn't support five million that way, let alone billions. But think about how they do it. There're laws. Responsibilities. Feelings of caring for people close to you. The need for recognition. A need to eat, a need for money and an occasional good time. All of these are like the rope at the theater that keeps everyone nicely in line. But you . . . none of it means a thing to a man like you. You could sweep it aside in a second! Understand what I'm saying? For you there had to be something else."

"Mother."

"That's right, Mother. She was killed in an auto accident in fifty-six, and I used her to give you guilt, Arcad. A feeling, which you could never escape, that you had done something wrong, horribly wrong, and that you'd have to spend the rest of your life making up for it, making sure it could never happen again. You had to have that feeling. Otherwise—well, think of Sterling."

"And you."

"Maybe so. But I'm not about to kill myself."

"I want you to help me remember."

"It's there. You can open it up yourself. But I don't think you've ever wanted to."

"I remember killing her. She wanted to change me, and I couldn't control myself—I remember how it felt!"

Nukhulls grabbed Arcad's shoulder. "Part of that was real. Even a four-year-old knows when he's being sold out—even if it wasn't her fault. I exploited the memory of that feeling and expanded it. I needed that safety valve, Arcad, just as much as you did. I feel something like what you must feel when I key on her."

"But you could have trusted me!"

"How can you trust what you're afraid of?"

"Maybe we should start learning." Arcad stood up, and for a moment Nukhulls feared an attack. But then Arcad simply extended his hand. Nukhulls clasped it with his own, just as the door opened to admit Duenos and a scowling guard.

"Splendid, a spirit of cooperation!" He turned to his escort. "You may go."

"Senator, my orders—"

"Will include foot maneuvers in the Mojave if you don't leave us. Return to your post."

"Yes, sir."

Duenos waited for the door to close. "How's the leg, Mr. Arcad?"

Arcad said nothing, but limped to his bed, by way of demonstration.

"Healing. Very good. And you, Bruce—are they treating you well?"

"Food's not any better, if that's what you mean." Nukhulls

had not been too surprised to learn that, although Duenos was ostensibly under limited house arrest up at the compound's residence, he seemed to have some authority in the present situation. No wonder: when a man's built like a bobber, he usually rises to the top.

"We owe this pleasure to what, exactly?"

"Bad news, I'm afraid."

"You've been cut off from your tortilla supply."

The senator ignored this remark; instead of replying, he took a pen from his pocket and examined it nervously, turning it over and over with his fingers.

"Bruce . . . Ah, they tell me they've analyzed the video tape of the broadcast."

Silence. Then, finally:

"Tell me about it."

"Things don't look very good. We know about the sub-liminals." Duenos shook his head. "Metro hospitals are still up to their windows in shock cases."

"And I'm supposed to feel guilty about it, right?"

"I wouldn't underestimate the seriousness of your position. So far, the public has been told that Al's death resulted in massive cognitive dissonance."

"They got out the elementary texts, eh? Hear that, Arcad, no credit! Oh well, Deliewe doesn't want to look bad."

"You're far too smug. They haven't been told because it allows them some leeway politically. The full story comes out tomorrow."

"What!"

"Bruce, the Western Region has seceded from the Confederation. Your broadcast will be considered an act of war. Tomorrow Deliewe goes on the air to read the constitution for the new Republic of Calinda. And to describe the preparations for our defense, should that become necessary."

"*Our* defense?"

Duenos appeared embarrassed. "I have been offered a post in the new government. Under the circumstances, I'm afraid

I must exercise that discretion which comprises the main part of valor."

"Figures," Nukhulls said with disgust. Another thought struck him, and he said: "What about the response in the rest of the country?"

"No word from D.C. yet. And the effect elsewhere wasn't as severe as it was here. This is Al's hometown, remember. But the level of outrage is high. The maintenance of civil order on the continent now rests with the Confederal government. If it chooses to fight . . ."

"Well, well, well, outrage is high, huh? Let me tell you something, Duenos, every one of those bastards would have done the same thing if they'd had the chance. And if it wasn't for your pal Sterling crapping out, they'd be rolling to D.C., kissing their own asses the whole way. So don't lecture me. When Houseman gets us out—"

"You don't understand, do you? A state of war exists. The instigator—yes, you—of that state is in the hands of the belligerent party. You're to be tried as a war criminal."

Nukhulls sat down. "They don't have the guts!"

"Listen. Deliewe, Brown, some of the others—they were personal friends of Sterling's. And Stassen is livid. His own plans—to make political capital out of the secession question—have been preempted, so naturally he's out for blood too. Aside from the damage you've caused otherwise, all of them hold you personally responsible for Sterling's death!"

"That's insane. The man went loose over his goddamned wife. How the hell can they hold me responsible for that?"

"Our friend Arcad is how. Oh yes, they've found out quite a bit about your past activities. And produced a witness—Sterling's butler, Rusty—who will swear to seeing Mr. Arcad push Kam from the tower over the house—"

"That's not true—"

"Cool it, Arcad. Duenos, get the hell out of here!"

"I only wanted—"

"Get out!"

Duenos seemed genuinely upset by the demand. "All right," he said sadly, "I'll leave you. Perhaps when reality sinks in, you'll want to talk to me again." With that he left, and Nukhulls jumped up from the bed again.

"That sonofabitch, I never did trust him!"

"You've got to believe he's doing the smart thing."

"Yeah, well, there are times when making a deal stinks." He halted at the window to peer at the heavy mesh screen. "God, if I had a screwdriver I could get us out of here."

"You want me to try—"

"Hell, you can barely lift your ass out of bed as it is. Then there's the alarm field, patrols, wire. We wouldn't have a chance." He turned away. "Anyway, maybe a trial would be good. They'll try crucifying us, but we can make 'em look bad, you and me, show the public how we're being railroaded. As if we're responsible for the way this country's fallen apart. But we've got to stick together. What do you think the press would make of it, you being dragged in every day drugged to the gills."

"I don't know about them, but I wouldn't enjoy it."

"No." Holding the grate, he hung his head toward the floor. "No, I wouldn't either. You got anything at all?"

"Nothing."

"Oh, Christ, I don't even want to think anymore!"

Arcad turned off the light. "Then why don't you get some sleep."

"Maybe you're right." He went back to his bed, tried closing his eyes.

"Nukhulls?"

"Mmm."

"I want you to know that I don't blame you for what you did. I can't thank you, but I don't blame you."

"Thanks."

"I won't forgive you, either."

"I'll ponder the philosophical implications of that one in the morning, if you don't mind."

Nukhulls could not tell a little later if the sound from Arcad's bed was laughter. Or merely snoring.

Everything was dark, and quiet except for the chirping of a few crickets. Neither of the prisoners had bothered to shut the blinds, so light from the kliegs mounted around the compound perimeter illumined a rectangular section of the floor.

Outside, in front of the dispensary, two of the regional guards, bored with night duty, shared a joint. Neither thought the noise they heard overhead was anything more than a windblown twig clattering off the roof. When they finished, they sat for a few minutes to feel the breeze against their faces, before returning to their posts.

Inside, Nukhulls turned over onto his stomach. Something had brushed his cheek, an insect perhaps. He slapped at it. Again something touched him, as hard and big as a beetle, startling him this time. He opened his eyes. Someone was silhouetted against the window, someone who wasn't tall, someone whose wavy hair looked almost like a halo in the white light. Not him, Nukhulls thought, it couldn't—

"Sterling!"

"Quiet! You want to blow six hours' work?"

This had to be a dream. But the apparition went to check the other bed.

"This is Arcad?"

"Yeah, but—"

"Shut your mouth! Wake him up so we can get out of here."

So it wasn't a dream—or at least if it was, Nukhulls was going along with it until it ended. He went over to Arcad, and shook his shoulder while cupping his hand over Arcad's mouth.

"You think you can do some running, partner?"

"Huh?"

"Something the matter with him?"

"He was shot through the knee."

"Christ almighty—"

"Don't worry, he'll make it."

"What's going on?" Arcad mumbled. "Who's this?"

Nukhulls did not want to risk any emotional outbursts from Arcad. "Somebody who's busting us out of here, that's who." He managed to locate Sterling again. "Okay, what's the scoop?"

Sterling handed him a can of shoe polish. "Put this stuff on your hands and faces. And get into these." He threw them each a set of black overalls, and Nukhulls started pulling his on over his clothing. Meanwhile, Sterling stared up at the ceiling.

"How did you get in?" Arcad whispered suspiciously.

"Through the vent up there. As usual, the guards all stand staring at the locks."

"I won't fit through that!"

"You won't have to." Sterling took off the pack he had on and rummaged through it. "Now where is that g d thing— ah! Here it is. Give me a boost up here, Nukhulls. Great." He held something long and cylindrical, which he fastened to the inside of the vent housing. Plugging in some wire, Sterling jumped back down, reeling it out to a spot near the rear entrance. Nukhulls saw a switch in his hand.

"You guys ready?"

"Yeah."

"Good. I'm going to jimmy this lock. Here, big man, when I give the word, press this button. Not before, got it?"

Arcad tensed; Nukhulls touched his arm to steady him. "Come on, kid, let's get out of here first and sort this out later." Sterling worked on the lock. Three quick moves and the door was loose. He held onto the knob.

"Now!"

They were suddenly blinded by flame as the huge roman candle ignited. Whistling madly, it arced above the compound and exploded with the sound of a 500-kilo bomb.

"Let's go!"

Nukhulls took the rear, pushing Arcad along despite his grunts of pain. Overhead, a flare sizzled at the end of a small parachute, and the attention of the entire garrison was directed at it. There were shots, and some crystal fire, but all away from the direction in which they were headed. Sterling picked a twisting path through the alarm field; at the wire, a couple of forked sticks held it up far enough for them to crawl under. And the perimeter fence was broached by a meter-wide hole that had been hidden by clumps of manzanita and creosote.

They were outside. Sterling had his hopper a hundred meters downslope from the perimeter. Nukhulls helped him pull the branches away from the bubble, which was already open.

But Arcad would not get in.

"Come on!" Sterling yelled.

"I'm not going with him, Nukhulls."

"Arcad, are you out of your mind?"

"I'll find my own way out."

"With a game leg, huh, pal?" Sterling pulled off the hopper control stick suddenly, whirling around to bash Arcad on the head with it. He smiled, then dumped him into the back of the machine. Nukhulls nodded. In ninety seconds they were over the ocean.

The flare had not hit the ground before Duenos and the garrison commander were at the main dispensary entrance. One of the guards, still a little stoned, and thoroughly rattled, opened the door for them and turned on the lights. The prisoners were gone.

"I didn't see a thing, sir, I swear—"

"Dios mio," Duenos said, breathing heavily. He looked at the can of polish, the abandoned knapsack, and the launch wire leading to the blast-charred vent.

"Who the hell could have done this, Senator?"

Duenos shook his head. "Only a ghost, Captain. Only a ghost."

12.

To avoid detection, Sterling kept the craft at a low altitude, flying a circuitous route that had taken them north through Marin, inland almost to Chico Ag Station, then south to Diablo itself. By the time they reached the valley, the sun had just vaulted the straw-colored shoulders of the mountain for which the area was named. Nukhulls looked down at cracked white ribbon that had been a major freeway bisecting the area, and he saw the domed theater. Arcad's old house was not more than three blocks away.

The trip had been a strange, silent one. Arcad seemed completely withdrawn, and Sterling was intent on foiling possible pursuit. The questions Nukhulls formed for himself over and over remained unanswered. Suddenly, however, Sterling nudged back on the throttle and turned toward Nukhulls.

"Well, I've got us this far, gents. Now, if you would be so kind as to direct me to Mr. Arcad's former residence."

Nukhulls was surprised. "Why there?"

"Close enough and far enough away, that's why. Unless you know of somewhere else. Arcad?"

The psychokinetic did not respond. Whether he was still aching from the blow to the head, or whether he couldn't accept this turn of events, he refused even to acknowledge the other two men. The memories were coming back to him, memories of that last night on Devil's Slide, rising like lurid colors of oil that foul the surface of a clear blue pond. He was no longer a free man.

Nukhulls was unable to interpret the silence, so he shrugged his shoulders.

"All right," he said, "I can show you. See the intersection a little north of the theater? Follow the road into the trees. There'll be a court to the right. Land in the cul-de-sac."

Sterling nodded and let the hopper settle to an altitude of twenty meters. "So. Our friend has lost the ability to speak."

"He's just groggy—"

"Shut up!"

"Hey, I'm only trying to—"

"Don't apologize for me again!"

"This the court here?"

Nukhulls tried shaking off the anger. Arcad could hardly be blamed for the way he felt. "Yes," he was finally able to say as their craft jolted down. "The pink house. With the plywood windows."

"Wonderful," Sterling commented. Little had changed from when Nukhulls had picked up Arcad in the winter. The weeds were taller and bone dry, and the path to the door was overgrown. The hopper taxied up the drive, where Sterling cut the inductors and popped the bubble. He got out to stretch. The day was already very warm.

"Ohhh! What a night. Well, guess it's home sweet hideout for the next few days." He pulled a cheroot from his coat pocket, lit it, blew the smoke skyward, then watched with an amused expression as Nukhulls struggled to aid the reluctant Arcad in getting out of the hopper. Evidently, the leg had stiffened considerably.

"You all right, Arcad? Yes? No? Well, gents, don't want to seem pushy, but we had better get set up in there before it gets too hot to move. Arcad?"

Nukhulls faced the magician angrily. "Lay off, got it?"

He raised his eyebrows dramatically. "Okay. Just trying to

snap him out of it. Tell you what, I'll go inside and you come in when you're ready." Sterling tried the front door: it wasn't locked. He disappeared into the musty darkness of the abandoned house. Arcad refused even to turn until the illusionist shut the door behind him.

"Bruce, let's get out of here. Now."

"I'm afraid he took the key with him. And you're not walking anywhere for a few days."

"I don't trust him. This whole thing doesn't make any sense! Showing up when everyone thinks he's dead, breaking us out of there—you think he's doing it because he misses us?"

"Look. We can't sort this out right now. Let's talk to him, at least. We've got nothing to worry about anyway. The parogen ought to be wearing off soon. You telling me you can't handle him?"

"I don't want to handle him! God—" His voice broke. "I want to be alone!"

"Shit—" Nukhulls began, halting when he heard a rustling in the weeds to the left of the drive. Both men turned to see an orange cat—a little more ragged-looking than before—bounding over to lean against Arcad's crippled leg. The change in Arcad's expression was like the parting of clouds after a spring storm.

"George!"

"I'll be damned," Nukhulls whispered, bending down to scratch the cat's ears. Arcad picked up the animal, holding him closely, underneath his chin, like a child with a stuffed toy. For the first time in months, it seemed, Arcad looked alert.

"I brought him back here to let him go. Figured he could catch mice enough to live on," Nukhulls said.

"You did the right thing. Come on, let's see if we can find something for this guy to eat." Without waiting for Nukhulls' reply, Arcad stepped inside the house. They found Sterling with his head inside the fireplace, trying to get the flue open. His hair and face were dusted with soot when he finally suc-

171

ceeded. He turned, frowning as he saw the cat.

"We're going to eat *that?*"

Nukhulls laughed. "That's George, and he's an old friend. Did you find anything?"

"A can of hash and a can of chickpeas. What's your pleasure?"

"Since we have a guest, why not both."

"All right." Sterling crumpled some paper, built a cone of kindling over it, then torched it with his lighter. Soon, bright flame crackled amid gray ashes and broken glass. As Arcad went back to his well to fetch a dish of water for the cat, Sterling blew on the fire until he had a good bed of coals going. When satisfied, he punched a hole in the top of each can with a little opener he had on a keychain, then placed both cans in the center of the glowing bed.

"Not bad," Sterling said, brushing soot from his pants. "For personae non gratae."

Arcad returned with a bowl of water. He set it down and George began lapping it eagerly. Then, very deliberately, he joined the other two and sat close to Sterling.

"Pump still working, eh?"

"Sterling," he said, his stare leveled at the illusionist, "we can cut the small talk. I want answers. You're on my territory now."

"So I am." Sterling poked at the embers with a green stick. "And I'm ready to talk. I've been dying to tell someone for months—it's the hardest thing about my line of work, actually."

"The illusion—" Nukhulls blurted.

"Oh yes, it didn't go quite the way I had planned it. Or the way I told you I planned it. The mechanics were quite simple, an extension of my original concept. The suit I was wearing had a layer of liquid crystal, which I could dial to a number of different colors. The script said gold, but I came out flat black: *black art* is the conjurer's term for the technique. My only worry was camera angles, but I managed to slip by everyone and make it back to the countermass, where a nice pressurized compartment had been set up. I changed to a technician's suit and joined in on the dismantling. I even helped bring the silver back to the shuttle!"

"But we saw what was left of you, your remains—after . . ."

"Mr. Nukhulls, I thought you'd be more reticent to display your gullibility. But—my 'remains,' as you put it, were simply the burned-up shroud which had been protecting me on my way through the silver. The whole thing worked perfectly, to my own amazement."

Arcad stared, unable to comprehend the flip manner in which Sterling related his treachery.

"Didn't you realize what would happen? Are you some kind of monster? Why? Explain that to me, why!"

"Before you accuse me, why not talk to your friend here? After all, without his interference, the reaction to my staged failure would have been less severe." Nukhulls appeared embarrassed suddenly, which no doubt pleased Sterling, who threw the rest of his smoke into the fireplace before going on: "Anyway, why should we bore ourselves with this whole problem of motives, and countermotives, when I have serious business to discuss with both of you—"

"I'm not interested in anything you have to say!"

"Let the man finish, for chrissakes—"

"It's good advice, Arcad, take it." Inexplicably, George padded over and crawled into Sterling's lap. "There, you see? One in the room with taste."

Arcad crossed his arms and said nothing further.

"Thanks. I'll start by saying that you had a good idea, Nukhulls, a very good idea, deficient only in its execution. But the concept is solid. You seem to recognize the fact that words don't make it anymore. They've been abused for so long, and for such rotten reasons, that people have been conditioned to disregard, or at least suspect, anything said to them by anyone outside the close family/friend circle. Which means, of course, that the political entity as we've always known it—

meaning, wishes communicated to a representative who translates them into action—is finished. Yet, the need for social order remains. How is that order to be maintained when the people refuse to trust and support the old-world politico with his clammy handshake and meaningless pledges?

"You know all this, probably, but I'll finish for Arcad's benefit. We are presently confronted with a pair of alternatives: the evolution of an anarchistic society—a contradiction of terms, in my book, and hence an unrealistic proposition, given the nonutopic make-up of our brothers and sisters; or, the imposition of the will of the enlightened few. That, of course, is an old idea, tested many times in the past, without success. The basic problem was, I'm afraid, the limited means of those employing it. Naturally, in any population there is always a romantic segment who can be swayed by a mythic ideology which masks the heavy-handed superstructure of the dictatorial regime. But for the majority not so taken, the tactic of control has always been fear. Make no mistake, fear can be quite successfully applied, in some cases with results lasting a generation or so. But fear cannot assure the success of any imposed order, simply because human beings respond in kind as soon as the weaknesses of the regime become apparent."

George closed his eyes, responding to Sterling's long strokes with the back of his hand. Nukhulls wondered how Arcad could stand this deliberate, unspoken method of sustaining their conflict.

"So what's the point," Arcad said with a growl.

"I'm just getting there. In this room, the three of us have the means and the knowledge to overcome the limitations I just mentioned. Me, I'm an old hand at manipulation. I know why people want to be fooled, and how to do it. Unfortunately, I've made a reputation in a field which doesn't mark me as a serious, concerned citizen, if you know what I mean—which is one reason I've made my retirement appear permanent."
He noticed steam escaping from the holes in both cans, and, taking the stick, he rolled them off the coals.

"Let 'em cool a bit. You, Nukhulls, are a master mechanic. You don't want to be seen, but you know the process by which people can be made to *aspire,* to want, to do. You know how to get inside them with that equipment of yours and open 'em up for whatever message suits you. In this case, the message you employed was not the correct one, but you really weren't all that interested in the message—am I right? You care only that your theories are proved, and, in light of what happened the other day, I'd say you have nothing to worry about on that score." Sterling tossed the opener to Nukhulls.

"See if you can get those open, will you? As for the owner of this beautiful feline: Please, you don't have to be so rude; I'm trying my best to be civilized, to forget what happened before. Incidentally, Arcad, you've got to get Nukhulls to tell what went on that last night." He raised his eyes toward the ceiling in mock amazement.

"Don't push me any further."

"As I said, civilized. Arcad, you are the ultimate facilitator. Shall I tell you what that means? You don't plan—in fact you're afraid of planning. You don't make moral decisions. You are interested only in locating A, locating B, and putting them together to come back with C. Except in your case, you can *make* A and B, or forget it and materialize C. A man of your ability is the perfect instrument, because no time is lost from instruction to translation. And as long as you're supplied with sufficient activity, you don't worry about ethical considerations." He smirked. "Not to stir the fires, but that's my own mistake. I wanted to plan and execute, just as Nukhulls did, and we both overextended our resources. With more or less equally tragic results. Say, hand me some of that stuff."

"It's not bad," Nukhulls said, biting gingerly into the steaming hash. "Arcad?"

"No," Arcad said, getting up. "I've heard enough."

"Don't be rude." Sterling gripped George around his neck. "Please, allow me to finish. I propose, gents, a coalition. Heads and hearts and hands. We have here in this country a very dangerous state of affairs, a very ripe state. The Brazilians have their greedy eyes on Mexico already. And the Russians are about finished licking the carcass over in Asia. They'll want their piece too. It's up to us to keep things from going completely to hell. We've got the expertise. We've got the power. And we've got money—that big silver ball that supposedly fried me to a crisp. So." Sterling took a final bite, wiped his mouth with the back of his hand, then stood up. "I want you to think about what I've said. I'm willing to forget everything that happened and start over. Talk it out. Right now, me, I'm going to see if I can find some wood out there. We might be here for a while." With that, Sterling walked out the front door.

Nukhulls eagerly scraped the last of the chickpeas from the can. He was filled with new vitality, struck by the concepts Sterling had outlined for him. Here was his chance to set things right again, prove that his method of control was practical. And to work with a man who thought the way he did! No more bureaucratic obstacles, shortsighted conditions imposed by politicians who were fearful of the opinion of "the people." He glanced over at Arcad, hoping that somehow the psychokinetic had absorbed the inherent validity of Sterling's proposition.

But Arcad only rocked on his heels, eyes closed, mouth clamped tight. Even George, flicking at a portion of hash with his tongue, looked disgusted with him.

"Well?" Nukhulls finally demanded.

"I haven't changed my mind. The man is sick. He talks calm and thinks storm. I'm leaving."

"Jesus! Arcad, don't you have any more brains than that after all these years! You're a wanted man! Where the hell can you go if you don't stick with us—can you tell me that?"

"The parogen's worn off. I don't think I'll have any trouble."

"So you go. What the hell will you do with yourself?"

Arcad sighed. "I don't know. There's a place for me somewhere. I'll find it and live out the rest of my life in peace."

"Peace! What the hell kind of peace are you going to have, knowing there's a war going on—yeah, that's right, a war—that you could have prevented—"

Now Arcad smiled. "The peace of knowing I don't have a thing to do with it."

"That stinks."

"Maybe so. But at least I'll know what I'm doing."

Nukhulls stared. "What about me?"

"What about you?"

"Our friendship. I took care of you, dammit, I built you! That doesn't mean anything?"

"Not anymore. You made a promise to me, remember, when I agreed to get into this thing. You owe me more than I owe you. And I discharge my part of the debt by giving you some advice right now. Leave here with me. You're crazy to trust that man. You haven't seen him the way I have . . . when he had the power. When he tossed his own wife like a damn rag doll right off that tower. The look in his eyes when he came at me. All Sterling wants is control—look, he's got you ready to do anything for him! Bruce Nukhulls, who prides himself on staying on top—"

"I'm using him—"

Arcad laughed harshly. "Using him! I'm sorry to say it, but you're out of his league. Come on, Bruce, leave with me. Sterling will find somebody else to mesmerize. But don't hand a loaded gun to a lunatic—the way I did at that party."

"Arcad, you're wrong. You'll find out, by God you'll find out, and when you do, don't come crawling back. Mother's still waiting."

"No." Arcad shook his head. "Not now. I could force you to come with me now, but I'll show you enough respect to leave it. We'll make our own decisions. Maybe the last we'll ever make."

Nukhulls kicked a can into the fireplace, and the noise sent George skittering across the floor for cover. "I guess that's it, then," he said, knowing that anger was useless.

"It is."

"You leaving now?"

Arcad considered. "No, I don't think so." He looked out the back door to where Sterling chopped away at a large stump with an ax. "Sterling's probably armed. I'm sure he won't let me walk away from here, so listen: I want to get some sleep before I go, and it's better if I travel at night. Tell him we agree. I'll be in the bedroom. Tell him we'll talk when I wake up. He's tired himself, so when he falls asleep, wake me and I'm gone."

"I don't know if I can do that."

"I'm asking you. For my mother, okay?" He looked at Nukhulls, and it took a supreme effort not to project his will. The other man scratched his head, finally, nodding his assent. Arcad hugged him.

"Save it, big man, save it." Shaking his head, he watched Arcad limp into his bedroom. George meowed by his ankle; Nukhulls bent to pet him.

"Yeah, boy, I know. What can any of us do?"

It was nearly an hour before Sterling came back inside; his clothing was soaked with perspiration, but otherwise he still seemed fresh. Nukhulls rose stiffly from the box he had been sitting on. "How'd it go?" he asked.

"Got a pile of split wood bigger than me. Should last a few weeks. Where's Arcad?"

"He's sleeping in there." Nukhulls wondered if Arcad might be listening in right now.

"I bet he does it on his tummy."

"You don't have to be snide. He's a good man."

"Yeah, I know." Sterling mopped his brow with the sleeve of his shirt. "Pure as the driven snow. So tell me—what did you two decide?"

"We—we'll go along with whatever you say. Partners— Say, what's the matter?" Sterling had not been able to hide his shocked expression.

"Huh? Oh, nothing. I expected more of a fight from your friend." Nukhulls looked at him curiously; his eyes were glazed, as if he was recalculating his position at forced high speed. The reaction made Nukhulls realize that Arcad just might be right about this whole situation.

"You haven't changed your mind, have you, Sterling?"

"No, no, it's great news. Listen. Let me go out and bring some of the wood inside. When I get back, we can sit down and start figuring out what we can do, okay?"

"Whatever you say, boss."

"Uh, yeah. Hold on." Sterling quickly disappeared around the side of the house, and it made Nukhulls edgy not to have the magician in plain view. Nukhulls was about to stroll out through the double doors leading to the patio, when he heard a loud thumping sound from the farthest bedroom, at the end of the hall. For a moment he thought it must be George— but the cat was asleep on the cool floor near the kitchen. And Arcad was in the first bedroom. He decided to investigate, walking softly to the closed doorway. There was something— the sound of muffled voices, he was sure—coming from inside the bedroom. Jesus, he thought, if I had a crystal now! But he didn't. Holding his breath, he pushed the door open sharply; in the dim light, he was unable to identify the figure standing next to the window.

Until she spoke: "That's damn rude of you!"

Nukhulls blinked. The woman, halfway into a long, silky gown, was none other than Kam Sterling!

"You! You're not dead—"

"For the grace of God, that's correct. Close the door behind you, please." She pointed the silver .45 from the party at him. He noticed that the weapon was now fitted with a silencer.

"This whole damn thing . . ." He shook his head helplessly. "It's all been a fraud, hasn't it?"

She smiled. "You catch on quickly. But not quickly enough. You ought to have taken Arcad's advice, you know. Al counted on that greedy streak of yours, but it looks like you've surpassed his expectations. You weren't supposed to see me yet. And I hate to spoil a surprise. So excuse me for not talking to you longer." Her features hardened, and she fired, the bullet slamming into Nukhulls just below his right shoulder. Blasted back against the wall, he slumped down to stare dully at the spreading blood sopped too quickly by his cotton shirt. Kam snorted once, walked past him smartly, and shut the door.

Sterling met his wife in the hall outside Arcad's room.

"You get him?"

"Good enough." She nodded in the direction of the door. "Still want to go through with it?"

"Damn right I do. I want that power for myself and we're going to get it. All set?"

Kam felt along her sides for the twin aerosol cans she carried strapped to her hips. "Yeah, these misters tested out okay. I'm ready."

"Well, be careful. I'm sure the parogen's worn off by now. Play off his grogginess, and remember the cue. As soon as I hit this door, you trigger the mist and get the hell out. Rattle him enough and we'll be home." They embraced briefly. Then Sterling stood back to watch his wife slip into Arcad's bedroom.

Arcad was sleeping peacefully for the first time in almost a week. Dreaming nothing in particular, he was half aware of the touch of a soft hand against his cheek and a warm voice in his ear. He stirred, and opened his eyes to the figure draped in silk.

"Arcad," she whispered, "why?"

He rose on one arm. "Kam. No, it can't—"

"Yes, dear. I'm with you and I'm staying with you. I'll take the place of your mother—would you like that, darling?" She extended her arms toward him languorously, coming close, filling the air with the memory of the scent of honey.

"No!" Arcad shrieked. "No!"

There was the kiss of fog on his face, coupled with a moment of swirling gray, as Arcad rubbed his eyes, fighting the tears that threatened to savage the peace he'd gone to bed with.

When his vision finally cleared, he saw Sterling standing at the foot of the bed with a concerned expression twisting his gamin's face.

"Where is she?"

"Who? Hey, you're dreaming, man. I heard the scream all the way out in the yard."

"I saw Kam!"

Sterling's eyes clouded. "I thought we were going to forget all that—"

"I tell you I saw her!"

"Arcad. My wife is dead. That's something we both saw."

"I—" He looked around, wounded and confused. "Where's Nukhulls? I've got to talk to him."

"Ah, well, that's something I was going to break to you when you finally did get up. He's gone."

"What do you mean gone!"

"Just what I said. Oh, it was my idea. He realized that you and I had some unfinished business to take care of."

Arcad was at the point of breaking down entirely. "I can't believe . . . I—ohh . . ."

Sterling seated himself on the overturned cardboard barrel that served as Arcad's nightstand. "Hey, get yourself together, friend. You want a smoke? This cannabis is guaranteed to calm anyone down." When Arcad made no reply, the illusionist stuck the rolled cigarette into his mouth and lit it for him.

"There, that's it, take a drag, you'll feel better. I'm sorry you're having these dreams, but in a way they lead in to what I wanted to discuss with you. Here, let me have that a moment. Ahh!" He blew the smoke out slowly, through his nose. "That's more like it. You feel any better?"

"No."

"Have some more, then. Yes, it's too bad you're burdened by your conscience, Arcad. If I understood Nukhulls correctly, you had just overcome your old—shall I say 'constraints.' And now you say you've been visited by my wife! A pity. With some elements of irony, I might add. See, I guess you could say that both of us are responsible, directly or indirectly, for some pretty bad things. But only one of us is guilty. I wonder if it's the right person in this case."

"What—what are you talking about?" Arcad asked, half-choking on the huge amount of smoke he'd just inhaled.

"Guilt is a very protective emotion. I mean, think about the way you've lived the last ten, fifteen years, running from the shadow of your mother. She became the persona for your power, and you carried her around in the trunk you made—your conscience. It's a trunk full of false-bottomed boxes with the power still tucked away inside. Guilt's very easy that way, even though it leaves the basic situation unresolved. Who killed Kam? Was it you or was it me? That's something you're going to have to deal with, Arcad. Think about it. Kam: every night for the rest of your life. No peace. Nowhere to turn. You want to die but you can't die. Is that the way you want to go on?"

Arcad sat with his knees pulled up to his chest. "No," he said, hiding his face between them. "But what the hell can I do about it?"

Sterling smiled a very careful, controlled smile. "We were equals once. We've had it out twice and split the decisions. There's only one way for you to free yourself, and that's to fight me again. As equals. Guilt to the loser, the stronger force survives. Yeah, that's right, shake your head, you know exactly what I'm talking about! No more doubt. No more Kam, I can guarantee you that. If you win, you'll be able to do anything you want without that guilt hanging over you. If not—well, what wonderful, fitting punishment for you."

Arcad's eyes were open wide, twin maelstroms of clay dust. "You expect me to give you your power back!"

"You won't be giving me anything I didn't already have, once."

"And what if I refuse?"

"You know the answer to that one yourself."

The psychokinetic considered: To have such a horrible choice forced on him, just when he thought he was free. He remembered the false impression of his mother's death, and what that had cost him for twenty years. Was he to spend the rest of his life with a different scenario, the rag-doll wife of a crazed magician dashed to an uncomprehended death atop the storm-lashed rocks below Devil's Slide? The smell of honey still lingered in the room!

Sterling was right. If he didn't restore his power, he'd never know if he was strong enough to prevail; never be certain if he had the right to go on living.

Somehow, he got to his feet. Tentatively he searched out the power center in the back of his brain, and found it energized and fully in control. Arcad wasn't entirely sure he could do what Sterling wanted, but if he could take power away, certainly he ought to be able to reconstruct it.

"All right, Sterling, I'll go along with it. I'll try to give you strength equivalent to mine. Then we can go outside and have it out to the finish—without pawns this time. Agreed?"

Desire crackled in the magician's blue eyes. "What'll I do?"

"Just try to open your mind, that's all. It'll be something like a hot template cutting plastic. Don't say anything 'til I tell you I'm done, all right? On two: One . . ."

Force streamed from his brain, an energized concept that rearranged atoms according to the requirements of Arcad's will. He felt Sterling's mind alter in a way that was unfamiliar—no resistance as before, and no change in the illusionist's expression, either, other than a reddening of complexion. Arcad was puzzled for an instant, then realized, too late, that he had been fooled.

Sterling had never had the power before.

And he did now. The bed rose from the floor until Arcad's head bumped the ceiling.

"You did it! You did it!" Sterling cried.

"How—you couldn't have faked it, I was sure—"

Kam stepped into the bedroom as the mattress slammed to the floor. "It was all your own projection."

"You're alive!" He made a move toward her and was frozen in place by the irresistible power of the newly charged Houdini. The distraction was all he'd needed. "I saw . . . you . . . die." Arcad was barely able to speak.

"You saw me go over the edge, darling. Into a net." She put her arm lovingly around her husband's shoulder. "We choreographed the whole struggle, and when you finally pushed— there was nothing holding me on. Damn near flew over the net, too, but I managed to survive."

"But the meeting at the warehouse—"

"That, pal, was a little of the applied psychology we talked about once. See, I knew something about your mother fetish. Our form—the one you were supposed to send down to disrupt my performance with—was purposefully modeled after your impressions of her. We hoped that the tension of the moment and the reminder of your 'murder' would be enough to fool you into struggling with a power I didn't have. The head of Harry Houdini was a projected hologram; I had an air line running up the collar of my shirt. Incidentally, your reaction had the added effect of convincing some of the dubious members of the Planning Commission, which was perfect for what I had in mind."

Arcad tried fighting Sterling off, but he was unable even to blink his burning eyes. Apparently, during the transfer Sterling had damped the capabilities of his erstwhile benefactor.

"Why, Sterling?" he gasped. "Why the whole play?"

"It's complicated—but basically, I was in a jam when you people showed up. I was committed to working for the July Fourth Company and certain influences were looking at me like I was a traitor. My original intention was to trigger secession, just the way it finally did happen. Your friend Duenos filled me in on you and Nukhulls, and what you had in mind. You could have wiped me out that first night, but you didn't. So I decided that if I could make you cautious enough, afraid of taking me on, we'd be able to get our plans for the illusion firmed up—which meant getting the commission to accept the broadcast. After they were convinced, the last step was to get you out of the picture entirely. Kam's bit in the water casket was perfect, wouldn't you say? After that night at the Slide, I couldn't see straight for three weeks. But it was worth it. I died as Houdini. The region has seceded. And I sprung you two in order to prevent your becoming martyrs, inspiring to the forces of the Confederation.

"And, of course, to see if I could force your power out of you. God, this is wonderful! Arcad, you've been an ass all your life, you realize it now, don't you—"

He broke off as George pushed the door open. The animal became upset when he saw Arcad helpless, and he howled several times before a kick from Sterling stunned him into silence.

In the other bedroom, Nukhulls lolled in a curiously cool, suspended state. The image of the dragon was before him, laughing at his foolishness. All that had been accepted, naturally—he was ready to go.

But he heard the faint sound of feline distress from down the hall, and the note of urgency revived him somewhat. He remembered who he was and what had happened. With an arm which seemed to be made of solid metal, he reached to his belt and nudged the hidden switch which activated his dead-man. There was no other weapon available to him. Somehow, he rolled over onto his stomach, and started inching his way toward the sound of the injured cat. The pain had gone from his chest; the dragon laughed no longer.

"All right, Al, what are you going to do with him?" Kam had lost a little of her nerve.

"He's put me through too much. Arcad, you sonofabitch, you're going to die the way you wanted to kill me. I'm going to rip you cell by cell—"

Nukhulls lay across the open doorway as Sterling brought up his power. He smiled as he felt the static crackling at the base of his skull. Sterling began to work. . . .

The dead-man went off. A single, crystal-clear beam straight through the head of Alphonse Sterling. The illusionist hung for a moment, the sick smile of comprehension fading from his lips. Then, suddenly released, he fell to the bed, with Arcad, slumping over the psychokinetic's body.

"Al! Oh my god, Al!"

Arcad looked up at her face, where her indecision showed. She couldn't settle on arrogance, or grief, or guile. The magician was dead.

As for the psychokinetic, he stood up slowly and saw Bruce Nukhulls dead in the hall. George got up, wobbling but otherwise not seriously hurt. Arcad looked down at Kam sobbing uncontrollably at his feet. He remembered the emotions he'd felt for her, the desire, the need to please. He remembered her treachery and her talent, and he decided what to do. Free of his guilt, he felt this determination to be appropriate.

"You deserve it, Kam," he said in a firm voice. "And so do I." He projected directly into her mind the exact force necessary. "Forget. Forget it all."

Gradually, she stopped weeping, straightened herself, and looked up at him with a pure, quizzical expression, tempered by a light playfulness.

"Who the hell are you?" she demanded.

"Not the other Houdini, ma'am."

She laughed, not understanding, but she accepted his hand as he pulled her up to her feet.